Another man might pass the garment off, or at least avert his eyes.

Not Ryan, though. No, he stood blatantly fingering the delicate trim of the thong with that nefarious curve to his lips.

The things she forgot. Like his admiration for lingerie…and high heels. Together.

Wear this for me…

Powerful memories that stole her breath and shocked her body into a state of desire it hadn't known in altogether too long. Yearning heat slid through her, winding a disturbing channel of waking awareness down through the very center of her.

No! Not now. Not after all this time.

Not *Ryan.*

She'd given him up. Let him go. She'd just filed for divorce! Of all the men in the world, he was the dead last one she could look to.

It would be crazy. Futile. Utter stupidity.

And yet, the rough, midnight sound of it sent a shiver coursing through her. And the certainty… it would be hot. Intense. Utterly incredible.

Fortunately for both of them, if there was one thing Claire had plenty of experience with, it was breaking a mood. "Sorry, they don't come in men's sizes."

MIRA LYN KELLY grew up in the Chicago area and earned her degree in fine arts from Loyola University. She met the love of her life while studying abroad in Rome, only to discover he'd been living right around the corner from her for the previous two years. Having spent her twenties working and playing in the Windy City, she's now settled with her husband in rural Minnesota, where their four beautiful children provide an excess of action, adventure and entertainment.

With writing as her passion and inspiration striking at the most unpredictable times, Mira can always be found with a notebook at the ready. (More than once she's been caught by the neighbors, covered in grass clippings, scribbling away atop the compost container!)

When she isn't reading, writing or running to keep up with the kids, she loves watching movies, blabbing with the girls and cooking with her husband and friends. Check out her website, www.miralynkelly.com, for the latest dish!

Books by Mira Lyn Kelly

Harlequin Presents® EXTRA
136—FRONT PAGE AFFAIR
108—WILD FLING OR A WEDDING RING?

THE S BEFORE EX

MIRA LYN KELLY

~ Tabloid Scandals ~

Harlequin®

TORONTO NEW YORK LONDON
AMSTERDAM PARIS SYDNEY HAMBURG
STOCKHOLM ATHENS TOKYO MILAN MADRID
PRAGUE WARSAW BUDAPEST AUCKLAND

Recycling programs
for this product may
not exist in your area.

ISBN-13: 978-0-373-52835-6

THE S BEFORE EX

First North American Publication 2011

www.Harlequin.com

Printed in U.S.A.

THE S BEFORE EX

To my sister Jena—for her endless support, love, humor, talkdowns from the edge, and stylish tips.

CHAPTER ONE

"Oн, my God, isn't that your husband?"

Claire Brady stiffened at the urgent whisper. An instant before, she'd been basking in the afterglow of a deal that, now struck, concluded her business for the next week—mostly. The gallery was too much a part of who she was to ever truly be put aside, even for a single day. But in that moment, her phone had been quiet, her mind at peace, her senses drifting with the gentle breeze as she'd absorbed the bustle and beauty of Rome's Piazza Navona while light circles, courtesy of a dishy Italian seated to her right, stroked over her palm.

It felt good. She felt good. And she'd wondered if maybe this time...

Well, so much for that.

She shook her head apologetically at Paulo, the dishy Italian under consideration, and then shot Sally, her best friend, assistant and perpetual alarmist, an emphatic *no*.

She'd known sharing the secret of her ex would come back to bite her, but balanced against the isolation of holding herself apart for so many years, Sally's occasional false alarm was a price she'd been more than willing to pay. Still, this was the third "Ryan sighting" this month alone.

"The man lives in California. The United States. Besides, if he were traveling abroad, we'd already know it," she promised with a nod toward the newsstand at the corner of the piazza.

When all else failed, fell short or slipped away, there was one thing in her marriage to Ryan Brady that Claire could count on. And that was the media keeping her abreast of every sordid detail of his liaisons, financial conquests and daily adventures. No waiting by the door with a cocktail at five for her. She had the world news to tell her how his day had been and with whom he'd spent the night. And in this case, she had it on reliable authority that as of fifteen hours ago, Ryan Brady had been meeting with his lawyer in downtown L.A.

Sally's mouth pulled into a sideways twist that suggested she wasn't convinced. Her gaze darted between the newsstand and the fountain across the way. "Hmm. But this guy really looked like him."

Sure he did. "Like the homeless guy at the station looked like that actor...Gerard Bu—"

"Hey, he could have been in disguise."

"Eating out of a Dumpster?" Claire tried to stifle her laughter, but then simply gave herself over to it. At the stubborn jut of Sally's jaw, she pulled her in for a quick hug, earning herself a good-natured pinch in the process. "Ouch!"

"Hey, maybe he's a method actor or something."

Laughter subsiding, she grinned at her friend and conceded, "Maybe."

She sipped her espresso, enjoying the rich flavor rolling over her tongue, and set the shot-glass-size cup back on the paper-covered table.

Their trip couldn't be shaping up better. Getting away was good for both of them. Sally, because she needed more of a life outside the gallery than she'd allowed herself over the last year, and Claire...well, the timing had worked out providing a convenient excuse when she'd rather desperately needed one.

Claire cast a quick glance over her shoulder toward Fontana dei Quattro Fiumi where its Egyptian obelisk needled the washed-blue sky above—not so much looking for Ryan in the crush of milling tourists, as perhaps hoping to catch a glimpse of this stranger who resembled him. Though as quickly as the thought processed, she pushed it back.

Seated in the shadow of the church of Sant'Agnese in Agone, amid the splendor of baroque Roman sculpture and architecture, the last thing she should have been looking for was a man who reminded her of her estranged husband. It wasn't a healthy pastime. In fact, it fell only one rung below "looking for men who resembled Ryan and were toting babies with them" on the ladder of exceptionally bad and self-destructive ideas.

She'd moved on. Long ago. Really.

And yet she couldn't resist one last sweeping glance across the piazza. Chalk it up to morbid curiosity, but she wanted a look.

Her gaze tripped from one lacking male physique to another without need to stop—not one of them could even remotely pass for Ryan.

Good.

Sally's brow smoothed as she shrugged back into her chair, snuggling beneath the outstretched arm of her date, Massimo. "Okay, maybe I was wrong. I don't even see him now. Sorry."

"No problem," Claire assured with a dismissive wave.

Only, there was a problem. The damage had already been done. Whatever mood had been set mere moments before seemed to have evaporated beneath the reminder of a life Claire had put behind her. As if to illustrate the point, Paulo's seductive caress moved from her palm to the pulse point at her wrist…eliciting zero response. Not that he'd exactly had her enraptured before. But there'd been *potential. Hope* that this tall, dark, Roman stranger would spark something long dead within her to life.

Only now, the whole interaction—them seated beneath the open Italian sky, surrounded by the throngs of tourists populating Piazza Navona, with Paulo doing his best to seduce her across a small outdoor table while his friend did the same with Sally—it seemed so contrived.

Obviously of another opinion, Sally giggled and leaned over to Claire, her fingers cupped around her mouth as she whispered in her ear, "Since we've officially transitioned from gallery business to pleasure, do you mind if Massimo and I take off?"

Claire pulled back, searching her friend's eyes for any doubt and, finding none, gave a quick shake of her head.

Massimo stood behind her, straightening his jacket as he issued a few words to Paulo before stepping away from the table with Sally's hand secured in his. Sally laughed delightedly, and peered back, "You'll be okay?"

Claire's smile broadened in response. "Of course! Go, have fun."

At Sally and Massimo's retreat, Paulo's voice rolled across the table between them. *"Ora bella, avete solo."*

To any normal woman on the planet his pleasure at having her alone would have sounded like sin on a plate. A temptation too tasty to ignore. But then, Claire didn't exactly fit the norm. Not anymore.

Meeting his smoky gaze with the clarity of her own, she sighed and pulled out the smile reserved for situations such as this one. It was cool and remote. Subtly off-putting without being overtly hostile. Just enough for a suitor to recognize the futility of his efforts, without actually insulting him.

It was a time-tested dismissal that worked—except Paulo remained undeterred.

Well, she'd warned him. And honestly, the stroke of his thumb over her captive limb wasn't anything she couldn't ignore. Eventually he'd get the picture. And in the meantime,

Claire had plenty to occupy her mind with the coup she'd just pulled off for the gallery. Faye Lansing had been a hunch. A bit of instinct and a lot of luck. The painting Claire discovered hanging on a bathroom wall—of all places!—in a client's home in Connecticut had been spectacular, leading her to track down the as-yet-undiscovered artist here in Rome. But that work had been nothing compared to what she'd seen at the studio this morning. Claire had scored Faye's first U.S. exhibit—and more than that, she'd secured her commitment to participate in the gallery's Young Artist Program as well. The kids were going to love her, and the way she spoke about her craft…it was pure passion.

She was so excited, and already sketching out a plan for an exhibit in the West Hall. With the interplay of light and color, that space would complement the work—

Suddenly Claire's attention snapped back to the present. To Paulo. And a touch that couldn't be ignored after all. What began at her palm had migrated to her wrist, and was now on the move again, stealthily advancing toward the crook of her elbow and, no doubt, beyond.

Distaste turned within her at the sight of his fingers slipping over skin numb to his appeal.

Hurt feelings or damaged pride weren't her intent, but if subtle didn't do the trick then she wouldn't be subtle. Resigned, she closed her eyes and braced for a blunt no-nonsense dismissal.

Only, in the next instant, the air around her changed. Charged with an electric current that rolled over her skin, bringing every fine hair and nerve to attention. Paulo's fingers stilled where they were, and Claire's eyes burst open as a strong, wide hand closed over her shoulder and smoothed into a possessive caress toward her neck.

"Hey, kitten. Remember me?"

Oh, God. Sally hadn't been wrong at all.

The air leaked from her chest in a groan, pushing the name poised at her lips free. "Ryan."

"Try to contain your excitement. You're making me blush." His gruff laugh, deep and darkly confident, sounded at her ear an instant before his lips brushed the tender skin beneath.

Claire jolted at the affront—definitely not from the tingling sensation skirting her skin—and instinctively grabbed for Paulo's hand as her defenses slapped up around her.

Where did he get off?

Twisting around in her chair—too uncertain of her legs' ability to support her to risk standing, she gasped, "What are you doing here?"

"I'm not letting you blow me off like you've been doing for the past nine years."

Claire's mouth dropped open, first from the aggressive edge to Ryan's words and then further as Paulo, taking her death grip as some kind of call to action, shot from his seat.

Oh, no. Not a good idea.

He might have Ryan matched in height, but something about the Italian's body told her his muscle was machine made. Gym buff. As opposed to Ryan's, which was all hard-hewn man. Rock climbing. Rugby. Water polo. Swimming, surfing, hockey and track. She'd seen the double-page spread of him in that magazine on men's fitness. And she remembered all too clearly how capable of defending himself—or anything else he felt possessive of—Ryan was. Only, Ryan shouldn't be standing there feeling possessive of anything. He should have been tucked securely away in L.A., watching the returns on his latest biotech-investment breed.

With one hand still resting at the crook of her neck, the other stuffed casually into the pocket of his charcoal trousers, Ryan cocked his head and addressed Paulo. "Take a hike. I need to speak with my wife."

Claire coughed, choking on his brass.

It had been years since they'd so much as laid eyes on one another. Who the hell did he think he was? "That's enough, Ryan."

All she needed was word getting out about the little legal matter that bound the two of them in unholy matrimony, and this quiet existence outside of Ryan's long cast shadow would be gone.

She wouldn't let that happen. Not now.

Paulo made a move to draw Claire to his side, but, sensing the tension building behind her, she gave a quick shake of her head then glanced over her shoulder. "No need for a public scene, Ryan."

In silent plea she stroked her fingers across Paulo's forearm. It was an intimate gesture, intended as much to appease her date as it was to send a message to Ryan.

Look at me. See how well I'm doing? See my handsome Italian lover?

Though as soon as Ryan left, she'd be working double time to worm her way out of the unspoken promise she'd just made—

Or maybe not.

What if she didn't shut Paulo down? What if she just forced herself to give in? *Do it.* Allow this man to seduce her. Would it be the hurdle she needed to get over in order to finally feel again? To be whole? Complete. She was so close to having everything she'd lost... Some days she couldn't even feel the cracks in this life she'd forged from the shattered remains of the one she'd had.

Her gaze shot the length of Paulo and back. Good looking by any sane woman's standards.

Could she ask him to make it fast, like taking off a Band-Aid? Probably not. But maybe once they got going, she wouldn't mind so much. And it couldn't last forever...

Decided, she extracted herself from Ryan's hold with an

irritated brush of her hand at her shoulder and pushed to her feet. Peering up into the dark Italian features in what she hoped was an approximation of adoration, she rested her palm at the center of his chest.

"Please, Paulo," she murmured. "Give us ten minutes to talk."

The smoky intensity drained from Paulo's face, leaving his expression flat. Hardly the sensual promise of a moment before.

"*Pietro*, Claire," he answered. "*Il mio nome non è Paulo.*" With a cool indifference that put her dismissive smile to shame, he plucked her hand from his chest, brushed a kiss across her knuckles and let it drop limp at her side before walking away.

Not Paulo? *Oh. Hell.*

Claire stood immobile, watching her childish stunt stride off in true backfiring fashion, keenly aware that the man who'd crossed an ocean to see her wouldn't simply evaporate and allow her shame to be swallowed in private.

No. Not a chance. Not Ryan.

"Wow, Claire. That was worth the flight over, right there."

Hostility welled fast within her. It was unreasonable. Intense. And directed at the man who'd barely had the decency to cover his laughter with a cough. She spun on him, fists clenched at her sides, ready to lay in. "Ryan! You jacka—"

Only she stalled barely out of the gate, stunned by her first full on view of the man who'd once been her whole world. Ryan. Tall, broad and tapered in all the right proportions. Strong chiseled features and firm wide lips. Sharp brown eyes that could be as unyielding as frozen earth or as warm as melted chocolate, glinting amusement beneath a fall of straight dark strands incapable of laying flat.

He was all easy confidence, smooth charm and gorgeous

man—everything she didn't need, standing there before her in the middle of Piazza Navona.

He shouldn't look so much the same. Not after all this time.

"Sorry about your boyfriend," he offered with a wry twist of his lips that was anything but apologetic. Another day, around any other man, she would have been laughing at her own stupidity in trying to manufacture a relationship for what purpose she couldn't even say. But around Ryan, she didn't want to laugh. She didn't want to revisit any common ground or shared entertainments. She didn't want to think about what it had been like once upon a time.

She just wanted to move on. Which was why she'd had the petition to divorce drawn up.

Shaking her head, she asked him, "What are you doing here?"

The amusement faded from his features and Ryan met her with a level stare. "Isn't it obvious? I'm here to bring you home."

CHAPTER TWO

CLAIRE blinked up at him, her sky-blue eyes betraying an instant of vulnerability and confusion. Proof he'd gotten past her guard.

Good. She'd sure as hell gotten past his. First, filing divorce papers without so much as a single word of warning. Nothing like getting served in your office lobby while juggling a laptop, twenty ounces of scalding-hot coffee, three newspapers, smart phone, two messenger bags jammed with files, and holding a blueberry bagel in your teeth. Yeah, thanks for that, Claire.

And then, with that outrageous settlement proposal. And in typical Claire fashion, flatly refusing the smallest concession. Leaving that imbecilic lawyer of hers to stonewall him, even after he'd rather magnanimously offered to meet and discuss the situation in person. Going so far as to pole-vault across the Atlantic to dodge talking to him.

But as if all that weren't enough, that first glimpse of her from across the square sure had been. She'd been sitting there in that legs-crossed, half-turned pose of feminine recline that extended all the right lines of a woman's body—hands moving animatedly with her chatter, smiling beneath the warm sun. *Smiling.* Bursting with life. So different from the fragile thing she'd been the last time he'd laid eyes on her. He'd never expected it. Hadn't been prepared for the sight of a woman he'd thought lost along with his marriage in a Boston emergency room almost nine years before. But there she was, radiant. Smiling while some lothario gave her his best go.

She'd tossed her hair over her shoulder in a simple, breezy gesture. One he'd always appreciated. The long strands came together like a fall of black silk streaming down her back, contrasting with the light complexion of her skin. Creamy pale but with a healthy blush of pink—and she'd laughed. She'd laughed and he'd felt it like the blistering relief of coming up for that first breath of air after a free dive.

And for a moment he was the guy he'd been when they met. Heart slamming in his chest as he ran off the track to chase down the girl whose lush lips had curled into that damn near criminal smile when he'd passed the stands. She'd knocked the wind from him more effectively than the six miles he'd just pushed through. And she'd kept him running, kept him chasing, until it was either have her or die trying.

Sweet, soft, sexy Claire.

Everything he'd wanted—and for a while she'd been his. He'd never burned so hot for a woman. Not before. Not since. But it hadn't lasted. Things had broken between them that couldn't be fixed. Claire had broken. They'd gone their separate ways and his priorities had changed. Eventually he'd gotten used to them being apart rather than together.

He'd gone on with his life. Done a bang-up job of it. But, seeing her again…she was too beautiful, and that *smile*—all he could do was stare.

And then that punk had gone and blown it. Pushing too hard and turning a smile Ryan hadn't even dared to dream of seeing again into the cold untouchable twist of lips that wasn't even in the same universe as what it replaced.

It made him angry. At the guy, at Claire. At himself for even noticing, let alone caring about it. She'd definitely gotten past his guard, but it wouldn't happen more than once.

Claire blinked again and with the lift of those thick black lashes all signs of vulnerability were gone, leaving a challenging confidence shining in their stead. "Take me *home*?"

He opened his mouth to clarify, but let it slip into a grin when she went on without bothering to wait for his response.

"Are you insane? On some medication? I'm not going to the corner with you."

"Keep your panties on, Claire. I'm talking about sitting down to work out a settlement. An *acceptable* settlement. Because there's not a chance in hell I'll let you get away with this."

He'd had enough of Claire's unwillingness to consider any perspective beyond her own. She'd wasted enough time already. Their lawyers'. His. And he was through sitting idle while she cut him off and closed him out. He wanted the settlement wrapped up. Packaged in a way where he'd be able to go on with a clear conscience. And since Claire clearly wasn't broken anymore, he was taking off the kid gloves to do it.

Arms folding across her chest in a slow, steady show of determination, she glared up at him. *"Let me?"*

Okay, that may have been a poor word choice, but when it came right down to it… He firmed up his own stance, letting his expression fall into its natural state of no-nonsense command. "Yeah, *let you*."

Claire stood staring up at him, her eyes widening with dawning recognition that he wasn't interested in game play. Or maybe not, because then those wide eyes began to narrow in what appeared to be shrewd assessment. As if she was… sizing him up?

Taking a deliberate step into his space, she glared at him. "I don't need you to *let me* do anything, Ryan. I haven't for years. In case you missed the news flash, I'm an independent professional who's built a successful career out of knowing my own mind. I know what I want. I know what I need. Just like I know what I don't."

She let the implication hang, the jab finding its mark without the benefit of voice.

"Yeah, kudos on the independent thinking, Claire, you've done a bang-up job with the gallery in New York. But I don't care what you *think* you want or don't want—"

"What part of *I don't want anything*, could you possibly find so offensive?"

Man, and now she was in his face and it was torqueing him off as much as that asinine settlement proposal.

"The part where half of what *we* have is *yours*! And you're going to take it." Jerking a hand through his hair, he punched out a heated breath. How the hell had she pushed him to lose it within less than five minutes of interaction? Screw it. He'd already chewed through enough time hopping continents because of her shortsightedness. He didn't have any more time to waste. "Look, I know you haven't dipped into that joint account since you finished school, and everything you've accomplished with the gallery was of your own doing. It took a lot of brains and a lot of savvy to do what you've done. But you're not using those brains about this."

The sharp edge of hostility in Claire's eyes shifted to an intense focus. He had her attention. "You're operating in the black right now. Earning impressive profits, but think about the swings in the economy. Think about your own life if you want a reminder of how fast some unforeseen event can change… everything. You've experienced it firsthand, Claire."

"I'd recover. Or start again. I did it once. And even if I couldn't, it's not your problem."

That's where she was wrong. He may not have known how to be the husband Claire needed, but he sure as hell knew about responsibility and obligation. Which was why he wouldn't let this go. "What if it's not the business? What if you remarry, have children? A dog? What if someone you loved needed more than your *independence* could provide? This isn't about you and me. It's about being practical. Doing the smart thing."

She'd winced at his mention of their past together. But hadn't even blinked when he'd referred to some threat to a future family. As if the point hadn't even registered. Damn, if he could read her.

"Fine, what if you *don't* remarry and something happens to you? Do you want to be calling me from some hospital bed asking for help?" He knew the answer was no. Just as Claire knew that no matter the number of years that passed, if she ever needed *anything*, all she would have to do was ask and he'd be there. The only problem was, Claire would *never* ask. So he needed her to take the money now.

Turning her back to him, she reached for her bag, pulling one strap over her shoulder as she efficiently dug out a few euros and then left them tucked under the small white espresso cup. What, did she plan on walking away without a word? To hell with that.

"The money is yours too, Claire, and you're going to take it. Because if you don't, you can forget about any plans you have of moving on without me. My lawyer's going to keep this tied up in court forever." Damn it, he was going to burn for this one. But, in for a penny, in for a pound. He'd failed her once, but he wouldn't fail her with this. No matter how belligerent she wanted to be, she was taking that money. "And he'll drag your gallery in there too."

Her body went rigid and then slowly she turned to face him. "You're a bastard."

"Yeah, I am," he agreed with weary resignation. "But I'm a bastard with your best interests at heart. Come on, Claire, don't fight me on this."

She blew out a long breath and smoothed the lines of her dress. "It's not like I have much choice, do I."

"No." But then neither did he. Not after all he'd done. But deep down, he knew, no matter how vast the fortune, it still wouldn't be enough to make it up to her. Nothing would be.

A couple at the far side of the café stood from their table, their conversation an animated, joyful exchange conducted in lively Italian that continued as they strolled off hand in hand across the square. They were married. He'd noted the rings—a habit he couldn't quite break—and the ease of their company. And he'd tasted that lingering bitterness that occasionally still took him by surprise.

Following their retreat, he let out a heavy breath. "I don't want to fight with you, Claire. That's not how it was with us. Not even at the end."

When Claire didn't reply, he turned back to find her watching him, her expression thoughtful. How long had it been since she'd actually *looked* at him? Even before she'd left, she'd stopped seeing him, her eyes so often drifting to some spot behind him or to the floor. Having her focus now…it was unnerving.

And ultimately unimportant to the task at hand.

Rolling a shoulder bunched with rapidly accumulating tension, he cocked his jaw to the side. He wanted this done. And done fast. He wasn't about to waste the ground gained by the gallery bluff. "The timing really couldn't be better. You've got a week free that happens to coincide with a lag in my schedule. We can have a settlement knocked out before next Friday. Who knows, if we really knuckle down maybe you'll have enough time to get back here for a day couple days before you go back to the office."

"This is my first vacation in three and a half years. I'm here with Sally. The timing couldn't be worse."

"You're the one who filed. I know you want this behind us.

To move on. The timing will never be convenient. It'll never be fun. But right now, it's workable. So what do you say?"

He reached for her arm, but she skirted his touch. Busying herself with her bag again, though it was clear there wasn't anything she needed. When she looked up, it was with businesslike reserve in the cool pools of her eyes. "I'd like to keep the divorce as quiet as the marriage has been."

"Of course." He'd worked hard to keep her out of the news. It had been dumb luck their relationship escaped notice at the beginning, but as the years went on he'd gone out of his way to protect her privacy. He wouldn't jeopardize it now.

"Which generally means openly referring to me as your wife is a no-no."

Right, that. He scanned the piazza in the direction Paulo-Pietro had strolled off in. "I didn't like that guy."

The corner of her mouth twitched, threatening what might have been the beginnings of a smile. "No, really?"

Really. He hadn't liked him—intensely and immediately—and even Ryan didn't want to examine too closely exactly why. He'd had enough surprises in the last day—no need to go searching for more. "You brushed the guy off and he ignored it."

"I could have taken care of it, though." There was no accusation in her words. Merely assurance. "I was about to. You don't need to worry about me."

Is that what he'd been doing? Before he'd arrived, the answer would have been yes. Definitely. Only, at first glance, it became clear Claire wasn't a woman who couldn't stand up for herself.

So if his actions weren't *protective*, that left *possessive*.

And that was just nuts.

Shoving his hands into his pockets, he nodded toward the street where his car waited. "Let's get this over with."

CHAPTER THREE

CLAIRE pulled her key from the lock and swung open the door to her room. Upon arrival the night before, she'd thought it quaint. A cozy retreat after a long day exploring the streets of Rome. But with Ryan's arm braced against the frame above her head, his big body only inches away, ready to follow her into the space…she saw it for what it was. Cramped. A claustrophobic shoe box jammed with a double bed, small dresser, nightstand and single chair in the corner.

"You don't have to wait for me to pack," she said with a cautious glance over her shoulder.

Ryan nodded into the room, hanging back until she'd cleared the far side of the bed before walking to the window. "I don't mind. I'll carry your bags down."

Wonderful. "Suit yourself."

Her cheeks flushed at her snarky tone, but the truth was, she resented the hell out of Ryan's railroading tactics—even if he did have her best interests at heart. They were the reason she hadn't wanted to get within shouting distance of him. Hadn't wanted to give him the opportunity to employ that subtle brand of strong-armed coercion that made him the wild success he was.

She hadn't wanted to be talked into a decision that wasn't her own, but in less than ten minutes he'd done it. And typical of his unique ability, he'd left her wondering how she hadn't seen his perspective from the start. It was infuriating.

When she'd begun pursuing the divorce, her goal was simply to sever ties. They'd both established lives of their own and, from her stance, there was no sense in demanding some portion of the assets she hadn't needed prior to the divorce after it. Then Ryan came back, batting aside her proposal with words like *unacceptable, misguided,* and *ridiculous,* and her response to that had been...emotional. She wouldn't discuss the possibility of an alternate settlement because she had a point to make.

She didn't need him. Didn't need *anything* from him. No more sacrifices, obligations or debts to be paid. Ryan had paid enough already. Too much.

But when he'd brought up the practicalities of the situation, she recognized her shortsightedness for what it was. And she'd been about to own up to it too before the jerk had gone and made that final threat about the gallery and keeping her in court for the rest of her natural-born life.

Her breath blew out in a huff and she threw open the closet door. Blouses, skirts, pants and dresses hung on the short rod, neatly organized by outfit and occasion. So much for that. Gathering everything into a single armload, she turned and dumped the lot onto the bed, returning to the closet for the luggage she'd stored at the bottom. She'd planned to stay a week, and now here she was packing up after less than a full day.

Irritating, but in the greater scheme of things, it wasn't anything she wouldn't recover from. And if it meant being able to finally close the book on that life they'd shared, then cutting her vacation short was a sacrifice she'd gladly make.

Efficiently slipping the hanger free of a washed silk crepe de chine top, she shot a glance at Ryan as he rubbed a hand over his opposite shoulder. The fabric of his tailored shirt pulled taut across the broad expanse of his back, revealing the flex and pull of muscles she used to massage at the end of a long day. He'd been in his prime then, but now, somehow he seemed broader. More powerfully built than he'd been at twenty-two.

A sharp pain bit into her hand, snapping her attention to the hanger jabbing into her palm and the blouse inadvertently mangled within her grasp.

She didn't like being this close to Ryan. She hadn't wanted to meet with him at all. Hadn't wanted to know what changes so many years had wrought in the man she'd once loved beyond measure. She'd seen the headlines. Heard the rumors. Hated the idea that he could be so different. And yet, here and now, a part of her was hoping everything she'd read was true. That the man he'd been was gone and all that remained was a body vaguely reminiscent of the one she'd known. It would be so much easier to defend this heart she'd painstakingly pieced back together against a body alone.

The pity of it was, she wouldn't even have to try.

Twenty minutes later, Ryan stood at the window looking out over downtown Rome, his back to the chaos erupting behind him.

"No, you heard me right," Claire grumbled into the phone wedged between her shoulder and ear. "He says two hours. Sally, I'm sorry to do this to you."

Yes, he got the point. He was the villain, inconveniencing everyone with his outrageous demands. Whatever. He was done with the placating and appeasement. Claire might not like that he'd cut into her vacation, but ultimately, she'd started the ball rolling with that fast pitch of papers. He'd just caught her off guard by being ready with a mitt and then calling her out.

By his count, they were even.

"Wait, when did the email come in...? They have instructions already on the East Wing exhibit. Drew has the insurance information too..."

The corner of Ryan's mouth kicked up. This was the fifth segue the conversation had taken back to gallery business in so many minutes. That after three calls on the taxi ride back from the piazza alone. Claire was as tied to her work as he was, and by all accounts loving every minute of it. She was good. Efficient. And decisive with a professional polish and an authoritative edge that hadn't been part of her makeup when they'd been together.

Gone was that pretty princess who was just a little bit spoiled but so very sweet he'd been rubbing his hands together at the prospect of taking care of her.

And gone too was the broken shell of a girl reality had all but shattered.

She was so *different*.

In some ways. In others...well, even his reactions were the same.

With her attention split between Sally and packing, he allowed his gaze to meander slowly down the length of her— from where the silky fall of her dark hair spilled over the too-thin, fuzzy white of her clingy sweater. The trim tuck of her waist and the filmy skirt that covered hips and legs he'd once known every curve and cut of, but now could only imagine, based on the hints revealed beneath the flow of fabric. And then there they were. Slim ankles, supported by the damnedest contraptions he'd ever laid eyes on.

Too many inches of slender spike to be safe strutting the downtown streets of Rome.

She leaned over the bed, one leg planted on the floor, the other cocked at the knee, toe to the carpet, heel swiveling in a slow turn.

Ryan swallowed, his mouth suddenly dry, his chest tight. Too many inches to be safe from him.

He was *not* thinking of the bite of that heel at his back. Or the way those legs felt wrapped around his hips. Over his shoulders.

Bad idea.

His gaze tracked up again, following the delicate turn of her ankle, the curve of her calf where it played a tantalizing game of peekaboo beneath the swaying hem of her skirt. Over round hips and a smooth spine that bowed into a soft arch as she reached—

Get a grip, Brady.

So being with Claire was nothing like the few times they'd shared space in the last nine years. Big deal. It wasn't like that first year either—when he hadn't been able to keep his hands off her. When everything was so damn right, before it suddenly, completely, went so damn wrong.

So what was with the leering and observation at a nonplatonic level?

Whatever it was, it stopped then. He'd made an international reputation for himself based on an ability to judge a situation or opportunity. Evaluate risk and return. And no good could come from letting Claire crawl under his skin.

A clatter of hangers over the bed snapped his attention back to the conversation taking place. "…a week, he says, to get the settlement worked out."

"Why?" A hiss of feminine breath sounded, easing into something that might have been a distant cousin to resignation. Her voice dropped, as though to mask an unwilling concession. "I want it over with."

A punch of guilt landed with her words.

Ah, Claire. Why did we wait so long?

But really, he already knew the answer. It was one he didn't want to think about now.

A quiet moment passed and then, "I'm glad to hear it's working out so well with Massimo—you know I am—but you've just met."

So Sally was staying behind.

"If you're really sure… Okay. No, that's great."

Fine with him. The fewer distractions the better. And maybe he wanted Claire for himself.

Not to drag her off to his bed. Hell, no. He was just curious about who exactly *this woman* was. Though he'd quietly kept abreast of her activities over the years, her endeavors and achievements, he'd done it with a few dozen layers—in the form of secretaries, lawyers, accountants and assistants—between them. Sure, he'd known what a success she'd become. Even if he hadn't seen the write-ups in the *Times*, the tax statements said it all. But all that was on paper. And the woman behind the profits and reviews—the one who had apparently been changing in ways he couldn't imagine—was one he'd insulated himself from.

So, yeah, he was curious.

"No, no. Sally, that's wonderful…I'm happy for you. I'll talk to you in a week then… Okay, you too. Goodbye."

Shoulder propped against the window casing, Ryan nodded toward the phone Claire had tossed into on open tote by the door. "So it's settled?"

"It's settled," she answered, assessing the mess atop the bed. "I'll finish here and we'll be ready to go."

He jut his chin toward the first overflowing case, making a point not to look too closely at the bits of brightly colored femininity strewn about in a haphazard mix with the other garments. "You need help with that?"

A distracted nod as she scanned the room. "You could close it for me and take it over by the door."

Ryan crossed to the bed and then, flipping the lid shut,

stared guiltily at the cotton-candy-pink thong that seemed to have sprung free at the last second.

It was tiny.

Delicate.

Sexy.

Cotton-candy-pink for crying out loud, and if he knew anything about Claire, it had at least one matching partner in crime buried beneath the clothes she'd shoveled into the case.

"Ryan?"

Hooking the slight scrap over his index finger, he held it up. "Escapee."

Claire shook her head in confusion. *Escapee?* What was he—and then she saw. Pink lace and silk, shimmering against the golden hue of his hand. Embarrassed heat rushed her cheeks at the sight of Ryan dangling her panties in a wicked taunt.

"Jumped right into my hands," he claimed, totally unrepentant. "What's a man to do?"

Another man might pass the garment off, or at least avert his eyes. Not Ryan though. No, he stood blatantly fingering the delicate trim with that nefarious curve to his lips.

The things she forgot. Like his admiration for lingerie... and high heels. Together.

Wear this for me...

A frisson of nerves rippled through her, spurring an odd clench low in her belly. The seductive echo from another time teased through her mind, spurring a hundred memories to life. Each flash of skin and heat more vivid, more dangerous than the one before—

Ryan taking her in the hall when they hadn't been able to make it to the bedroom three feet away... In the kitchen...the closet...the car...

Powerful memories that stole her breath and shocked her

body into a state of desire it hadn't known in altogether too long. Yearning heat slid through her, winding a disturbing channel of waking awareness down through the very center of her.

No! Not now. Not after all this time.

Not *Ryan*.

She'd given him up. Let him go. She'd just filed for divorce! Of all the men in the world, he was the dead last one she could look to.

It would be crazy. Futile. Utter stupidity.

Ryan flipped the renegade lingerie in his palm, offering it to her as the deep brown of his eyes held her captive. "Pretty." It was a single, simple word. And yet, the rough midnight sound of it sent a shiver coursing through her. And the certainty… It would be hot. Intense. Utterly incredible.

What was the matter with her? An hour ago she'd been ready to go toe to toe with this man, and now…now she was ready go— No! She needed to look away, get off the path of destruction on which she'd suddenly found herself—and before it led them both to a place that couldn't end in anything but embarrassment, the inevitable frustration she knew all too well and more of the guilt neither of them needed.

Fortunately for both of them, if there was one thing Claire had plenty of experience with, it was breaking a mood. "Sorry, they don't come in men's sizes."

Ryan gave in to a bark of laughter. Pulled the garment just beyond reach as she grabbed, then caught her wrist. She shuddered at the heat of his hand winding up her arm, snaking through her system and pushing her heart into a staccato beat that pulsed…everywhere.

The amused smile died on his lips and the stillness of the room hovered around them. The fingers circling her wrist tightened, held firm, pulling her closer until only an inch of charged air separated their bodies. His brow drew down and a harsh question darkened his stare.

There was nothing she could do. No place to hide.

No more playful banter between them, quick comebacks or easy laughter. Just the stretch of silence. Building tension. And Ryan's eyes trailing a hot path to her mouth.

Everything slowed. Went warm. Heavy.

Her lips parted.

Good God, this was *Ryan*. This was *her life*. The one she'd struggled and scraped and so slowly, painstakingly rebuilt. A life too precious to risk on *rash* or *impetuous*.

"Sorry," she managed to say on a shaky breath. "No souvenirs."

Ryan blinked, his hand jerking loose from her wrist as if he'd been burned.

Well, he had. They'd both been burned. Years ago. An ocean away. A lifetime before. And neither of them were fool enough to play with that kind of fire again.

CHAPTER FOUR

CLAIRE stared out the back window of Ryan's chauffeured car, following the cut of highway through the Southern California valleys. At either side land swelled in green hills dotted with homes, palms, brush and the frequent sandy scar of sheered-off earth. It was beautiful even with the gray wash of inclement weather darkening the landscape and early-evening sky.

Somehow the gloomy weather seemed fitting. As if it held a sullen, quiet kind of ache in the air. No stormy, tumultuous hurricane or even weepy rain. This was simply a touch of melancholy, an apropos backdrop to the conclusion of a marriage that had, for all intents and purposes, ceased to be years ago.

The sound of a clearing throat drew her attention back to the man seated across from her in the car. Ryan reclined in a long-limbed sprawl. Tie loose and slightly askew, top button open at his neck, shirt sleeves rolled to mid forearm where they folded behind his head. His laptop was still open beside him—an array of files cluttering the seat beyond—giving the impression that his break from work was intended to be as brief as hers. "So, what do you say we give the conversation thing another go?"

Leave it to Ryan to lay it out on the table.

The communication between them had been limited to a few stilted exchanges following that one charged moment in her hotel room. The one she was working overtime to put out of her head, but, defying her efforts with the tenacity of a garden weed, had given root to a thousand questions Ryan was the absolute wrong man to help her answer. By unspoken mutual agreement they'd taken refuge in work during the long hours of the flight. Though, somewhere over the Atlantic those questions had spread through her consciousness, seeding thoughts of repercussions and what-ifs and no-ways until they'd tangled to the point that business became impossible to focus on…and she'd found her gaze drifting across the buttery leather and walnut interior of the luxury cabin, her gaze roving over the details of Ryan's powerful physique. Wondering again, why Ryan? How, after so many years?

More than once he'd caught her staring. Their eyes would hold as if in quiet challenge. Each testing the strength of a disconcerting connection lingering between them, and their ability to withstand the spatial intimacy that was the ironic prelude to the dissolution of their marriage. And then he would look away, or she would. Without a word they'd return to the solace of their work.

Only spending the next week in silence wouldn't get the divorce finalized. So here Ryan was, making the communication happen.

Who was she to stand in his way? "What do you have in mind?"

His head rocked from one side to the other as he let out a rush of breath, considering. "Let's take it slow. Weather seems safe."

Claire swallowed, fighting to keep the twitch at the corner of her mouth from giving in to a grin. "Polite."

"Superficial."

"Benign," she offered with a little wave of her hand, amused by the preliminaries of selecting a suitable topic for discussion.

"Mundane. But what the hell…" He yawned with an indifferent gesture toward the window. "It's a shame you're seeing the place like this. Two days ago it was gorgeous. Sun shining, temps up about seventy-five. This time of year the weather can change on a dime."

Mundane was right. There'd been a time when they'd made a habit of talking the whole night through. When conversation between them was so compelling it physically hurt to end a call or say good night. To her recollection the weather had played into their interaction only once. A quiet Sunday morning in bed. Ryan's strong hands running soft across her hips as he pulled her astride him, describing in exquisite detail how he wanted to make love to her in the rain. What the scattered beads of water would look like across her breasts, how the cool chill of them would make her nipples tight, hard, achy… and the hot contrast of his mouth as he closed over her, licked and sucked, would make her moan.

Her nipples puckered as the memory of Ryan sliding hot and hard inside her racked her body and stole her breath.

Oh, no. Not good.

Suddenly, the weather seemed a threat beyond compare and Claire was anything but amused. She didn't want to think about how it had been. She didn't want to react to the point where it was taking every ounce of will not to squirm in her seat.

Rubbing her temple with two fingers, she stared at her knees, wondering how she could still feel the sheets beneath them.

"Your turn, Claire."

The combination of her name and the unsubtle snapping of fingers jerked her attention to Ryan's eyes steadily focused on her. Waiting, watching, studying her with an intensity that did nothing to diffuse the slow, stirring heat deep in her belly.

God, what did he see?

She needed out of this car. Away from this man before he caught on to the wet, rain-soaked direction her thoughts had taken or how shocking her response to them truly was.

"H-hotel," she stammered stupidly, immediately wanting to slap her forehead in the hopes of jarring her brain loose.

Ryan looked out the window, scanning their surroundings, and then back to her again. "What?"

"The hotel where I'm staying," she clarified, managing a "silly me" roll of her eyes, though there was nothing silly about how she felt. Desperate, more like. Confused. "Just drop me on the way in. I'll get settled and then—"

"No hotel," he cut in with a dismissive wave, his brow smoothing in understanding. "You'll stay at the house."

He couldn't be serious. "That's not a good idea."

"Sure it is. There's a small day staff to clean and shop while we're there. Don't be surprised if you don't see much of them. They've got a knack for being conveniently absent and yet amazingly available. Anything you need, they'll get. And I've got a car for you in the garage."

"No." The single word snapped out with more force than she'd intended, but suddenly she felt cornered. After spending hours trapped in close quarters together, the only thing that had kept her from bursting out of her skin had been the promise of having some time to herself. Knowing she'd be able to get away. Have a private refuge from her body's disconcerting reaction to the proximity of his. A place where the subtle, sexy, masculine scent of Ryan didn't permeate every corner of the space she inhabited, as it had for the last dozen hours of travel.

And that was before he'd gone and brought up *the weather*!

No way. Trapped in his house, she'd be breathing him in for seven days straight.

"Not even willing to discuss it, Claire?" Ryan asked, irritation evident in his tone.

She turned to him, striving for a calm that threatened to slip fast from her grasp. "We're hashing out a settlement—even under the most amicable terms, by the end of the day I'd imagine we'd both appreciate having some distance between us. Being able to unwind without the other there breathing down their neck."

Ryan's lips twitched at one corner and then pressed flat as he turned to study the passing terrain. "So it's the neck breathing that's the problem then. And here I'd always assumed you enjoyed it as much as I did."

Oh, that was perfect. A little sexually charged banter between them. Just what she needed.

Not.

Eyes fixed on the roof of the car, she shook her head. "You never change."

"Everybody changes, Claire. And everyone stays the same." He drew a deep breath, and let his head fall back against the rest. "It's just not always easy to see exactly how, is all."

The suggestive teasing tone of a few seconds before was gone.

No doubt he recognized how utterly out of place it was in an exchange with the woman he was divorcing, and packed it away for a more appropriate partner.

Easing back against her seat, she thought about what he'd said. About the changes between them.

He was right, of course. In too many ways, the man seated across from her wasn't the one she saw when she let her mind's eye search for her husband's face in her memories. The one who jogged the streets of downtown Chicago with that deceptively easy stride of a natural athlete, or sprinted the steps of their Boston walk-up, dressed sharply in suit and tie, working his pitch for some meeting or another. In her mind, he was forever the man he'd been, burgeoning with boundless optimism and ideas. A visionary yet to hit success. Young. Enthusiastic. And so gentle and tender, it made her heart ache to remember what it felt like to be on the receiving end of that kind of care.

Ryan was a multibillionaire now. Riding around the globe in his sleek private jet. So smooth and cool. No more nerves. No more pitches. Not since the *Journal* had started calling him Midas and the world at large began lining up to pitch *to him*. But that was just success. A surface change, like the deepened lines and furrows around his mouth and eyes.

Inside? She couldn't say. There were a few obvious things. He was harder now. More callous. Cynical. But beyond that basic awareness, she didn't know him. Didn't know if she wanted to.

And she imagined Ryan felt the same way.

Looking past her hair and eyes, he probably couldn't even recognize the girl she'd been.

But then, there wasn't much left of that girl now.

At eighteen years old her wants, hopes and dreams had been painfully simple and completely revolved around Ryan. She'd barely known her own mind back then. Hadn't even tried to figure out all there was to her. She'd been about looking pretty. Having fun. Laughing. Music, parties, clothes, shoes and dates. She'd enjoyed school, done well at it. But she'd been a freshman and hadn't had the time to find her niche before circumstances required her to drop out and everything changed so completely. When her parents discovered how she'd let them down, and all the love and support that, to that point, had been the foundation for her life was suddenly revealed as conditional.

She'd been so grateful to Ryan for being there for her. Standing by her. He'd taken care of her. Loved her. Married her. Brought her with him when he'd moved for his career.

He'd treated her like gold, but she'd treated herself like some kind of accessory to his life, rather than an equal partner in it. So dependent on him she'd been afraid to step outside his shadow. So in love she'd convinced herself he was the only thing she needed.

A prickle of buried resentment pushed to the surface, making her glance guiltily away. It wasn't fair to blame him because she'd been a fool. Or because he'd had another life to fall back on when the one they shared together crumbled.

She'd learned her lesson though. The woman she was now didn't depend on anyone but herself. With the life she'd built, she didn't have to. Where the old Claire had been content to drift, the new Claire was driven. Relentless in her determination. Tireless in her pursuit of her goals. Strong. Self-made and self-sufficient. The kind of woman a man accustomed to controlling every aspect of the universe around him wouldn't be able to stand.

Ryan closed his laptop, stacked the folders and stuffed them into the messenger bag at his feet. "Look, Claire, there's an entire guest suite. You can avoid any and all neck breathing. But we've got to get through this stuff. The house is nice. Trust me."

A guest suite wouldn't be enough. "I'm sure it is, but that's not the point. I need my own space. Room to work. You aren't the only one with a business to run."

"You're on vacation," he countered smoothly, though she couldn't miss the flinty edge in his eyes.

He didn't like being challenged, and so far that's all she'd done.

"That was more for Sally's benefit than mine, and since she's not around, I won't have to sneak off to keep up with the work I've got." She let out a steadying breath and searched his face for understanding. Found only a will she'd rarely had need to defy.

"So we'll be working out the settlement around our other obligations. Working early, working late, working whenever we can make it happen. It'll be easier if you're available."

Sure. His beck-and-call girl. That wasn't going to happen.

"I'll have an office set up for you in the house." Pulling his phone from his pocket, he swept a thumb across the screen. "Just tell me what you need—"

"A hotel, Ryan."

He remained silent. It was a tactical move in a power game she wasn't interested in playing. "You really do always get your way, don't you?"

Ryan held her stare, until the challenge between them dissolved.

"No, Claire. Not always."

She swallowed down the desire to find out just what he meant by that, and straightened her spine instead. "Good. Then this won't come as too hard of a blow." She wasn't giving in. And it was as much about self-preservation as it was about pride. "You're not getting it now."

CHAPTER FIVE

MINUTES later, her eyes wide with stylistic appreciation, Claire walked through the front entrance of Ryan's La Jolla Shores beachfront home. She'd be staying at one of the local hotels as soon as the room could be booked, but she had agreed to view the alternative. Ryan hadn't overstated the place. It was immense.

Three stories of slate gray, steel and glass stretched from a gated driveway, through a lush private garden, and back to the sandy expanse of beach it butted against. The architecture itself was masculine to the extreme—all clean lines and open spaces, suspended stairwells and stone floors. But the interior colors and decor were anything but minimalist or stark.

A vivid array of hues taken from the ocean and setting sun adorned each room in bold contrast and yet flawlessly matched perfection. And the artwork was spectacular, blending ancient Eastern and modern European with an eclectic mix that spoke volumes about style and taste.

The floor plan through the center of the house was primarily open layout, offering unobstructed views of the ocean from the main entrance, living room, kitchen and bar, with a few walled divisions to the left side. Because the house was built on a gradient, what had been the ground level at the front door was actually the second floor, resulting in the illusion that the terrace floated above the ocean beyond.

"This is stunning, Ryan."

He stood at a floor-to-ceiling wall of windows and grinned. "It gets better. Let me show you."

Releasing one latch after another, he swung the wide glass panels ninety degrees on their axis and turned the living room into an extension of the terrace beyond. A cool, briny breeze wound through the house, carrying the low rumble of waves, and catching the creamy sheers in a billowing dance of light, motion and sound.

Ryan nearly bounced on the balls of his feet, his obvious pride and pleasure in his home making him look ten years younger. "Pretty great, huh?"

Yes. Enough that she was aching to knot her hair on top of her head, stretch out her arms and let that delicious breeze tickle the back of her neck and tease through her clothes. Instead, she simply nodded her agreement with a genuine smile. "It is."

"So, kitchen, dining room and living area are here on the main level. My rooms are on the third floor. If you'd like to clean up before we get you into a hotel, I'll show you the guest suite."

Downstairs, Ryan held open the last door on the left, revealing a sitting area, full bath, bedroom and yet another spectacular view of the ocean beyond. Drawn by the opulence of a suite she imagined remained largely unused, she walked toward the back, by habit cataloging each piece of art and elegant adornment along the way. His collection was spectacular.

The bedroom opened to a second, lower terrace, partially shaded by the one above. Crossing to the window, she wondered how Ryan was able to accomplish any work with views like these available from every vantage in the house.

And then she remembered. "You don't really live here, do you?"

He stood against the far wall, arms crossed over his chest. "No. It's more of a retreat. I split most of my time between Boston and L.A., but I thought we'd be better off down here. Less visible."

"Trying to keep me hush-hush?" Claire teased with a crooked smirk, knowing full well the accommodation was entirely for her benefit. She was the only one with something to lose if their relationship became public knowledge. "Am I your dirty little secret?"

"Right," he answered with a short laugh. "Think how my reputation would suffer if news of my scandalous child bride got out."

"I was eighteen."

Another bark of laughter. "I should have been shot."

Ah, the old argument. Only this time, rather than give in to the usual go-round, she felt the need to voice her feelings while she still had the chance. "Hey, it was good for a while. We were both just…naive."

The lightness of the moment was gone as quickly as it had come. Ryan's dark brown eyes fixed on hers, then shifted out toward the horizon. He didn't believe her. But then, they both knew why they'd married in the first place. Despite how she'd wished it were otherwise, the marriage had been an honorable act. Ryan doing the right thing by her.

"Yeah, we were."

The words were simple enough, but there was a hollow, almost desolate, quality to them that pulled at the places in her soul Claire didn't like to revisit. And just like that, the memories were there. The good, the bad, the bitter and heart-breaking. Turning heavy and dark, they swamped her with emotions she no longer acknowledged. Weighted her shoulders with echoes of the bleak despair that had nearly stolen her life.

No. She wouldn't give in again.

Her vision swam and she took an unsteady step back from the glass, felt the ground give and the world go thick and slow.

"Claire!" And then Ryan was there, one hand clamped tight around her upper arm, the other locked across her waist as he caught her to him.

Awareness returned in a breath-seizing crash at the press of his chest, hips and thighs against her back. The solid strength of him bracketing her body. Pieces of a puzzle long ago abandoned, coming together in a dangerous alignment of hard and soft.

Her equilibrium returned and she steadied her footing.

"God, I'm sorry," she managed to say weakly, trying to step free of the arms enveloping her, but Ryan held fast. "I'm okay."

"Like hell." The gravel-rough words hit her ear, low and accusing. "What happened?"

Wondering the same, she drew a shallow breath. Then another. Deeper. Only, the next breath met the rhythm of Ryan's and set their bodies into synchronized movement that was... intimate. Her gaze dropped to her abdomen where Ryan's hand splayed low and wide, securing her to him in a hold that was almost erotic. She closed her eyes to it, but she could still feel the heat of his hand against her, the strength of his body behind. Remembering his hands moving over her the way they once had. One cupping, plucking at her breast...as the other slid lower to where achy heat had now begun to throb between her legs.

God, this was crazy.

No, *she* was crazy. Because it wasn't the memories causing her to sway on her feet. It wasn't Ryan or the past or the present or any kind of emotional weakness. It was her own stupidity.

"I should have eaten on the plane." Had some water. Slept

a little. But then she'd been too keyed up to register the basic needs of her body.

"Food?"

A harsh breath sounded above her head, and in an abrupt shift, Ryan swung her into his arms and carried her the few steps to the bed, depositing her without finesse.

"Stay there."

Ryan took the stairs three at a time, rounding the second level in a matter of seconds.

Food.

He'd nearly had a heart attack when Claire stumbled back on legs that looked as if they'd gone to jelly beneath her, her features slipping from that irritatingly controlled mask she'd been giving him to lax. Through reflex alone, he'd caught her against him before the reality of what was happening registered in his brain. And then she'd been in his arms and his blood stopped cold in his veins.

He'd been there before. Helpless. A bystander as the woman who'd been his wife bled from the body in his arms.

But that wasn't what was happening now. Claire hadn't eaten. When he thought about it, she hadn't slept either. She'd been a workhorse for that gallery of hers, keeping pace with him through their entire day of travel. But then, not only had he eaten, he was also accustomed to pushing through more hours than these. Did it on a regular basis.

What Claire was used to, he had no idea.

He should have paid more attention on the flight.

Only, every time he'd looked too closely at her, he found himself wanting to reach out and touch. To test the texture of her skin. See what she felt like again.

Well, he'd had his chance. He'd had her in his arms and now he knew. She felt good. So good that when she'd regained her senses and he should have let her go, he'd held on. Stealing those extra seconds of contact—

Shaking loose the fists balled at his sides, he held them out, assessing their steadiness. Swore and shook them again before wrenching open the door to the Sub-Zero.

No more touching. That was for damn sure.

A minute later he was back in the guest suite twisting the cap free from a sports drink and thrusting it into Claire's hand. "First this."

"Thank you." She turned the bottle in her hands, scanning the label before bringing it to her lips to drink. Several swallows later she rested the bottle against her knee and accepted the energy bar he'd opened.

He watched her eat. Followed each dainty bite until the pink tip of her tongue swept across the swell of her bottom lip to capture a stray crumb... And then he looked away. Willed the tightening in his groin to cease, calling up memories of the vegetable drawer in his college apartment as a last but amazingly effective resort.

"Feeling better?" he asked, tracking the empty stretch of damp packed sand to where it curved off into the cove. He needed to run. To push past his endurance and find that state of grace where the tether between mind and body stretched taut and thin. Where the world reordered in his head. And the tension twisting around his every nerve slipped loose.

"Yes... Just embarrassed more than anything."

He turned back to her. The color had returned to her cheeks and her eyes were clear and alert. "Does this sort of thing happen often?"

"No. Not at all."

That was a relief to hear, but at the same time, what if it was something more serious than a nosedive in blood sugar? Or what if she wasn't being straight with him?

He didn't know anything about her anymore.

Catching her chin between finger and thumb, he tipped her face to his, searching for signs of wear. Maybe a longer-term hunger or extreme fatigue. Anything to suggest things weren't as she'd said.

But upon closer inspection, he saw there were no signs of the gaunt shadows and sallow pallor that had haunted so many of his nights. Her features were a delicate balance of soft curves and attractive angles. Her skin was smooth. Her hair glossy and thick. Her eyes bright. Sure, there were faint shadows beneath, in line with what he'd expect from a day that had gone on too long, but nothing like the deep bruising of extended sickness. She was healthy, with a rosy blush to her cheeks.

A blush that was darkening with every unsteady breath—

—Because he'd been following the path of his study with the pad of his thumb. Perfect. So much for not touching.

He needed to get her out of there. Get that hotel room she'd had the good sense to demand, and put a half mile or more of space between them before he did something monumentally stupid. Like spend another second with his hands on her, staring down into her wide eyes, or brushing his thumb across that elusive line between lip and skin…to the center of that lush bottom swell he really needed to look away from…

A slow primitive drum beat the blood through his veins as awareness tightened its hold on his body.

Her lips parted, revealing the barest hint of her neat white teeth, and her tongue pressed behind. He could sink into that mouth. Cover it with his own. Coax her open, push inside and…taste.

Only, this was Claire and a taste wouldn't be enough.

Hell, he was being a damn fool. *This was Claire*, the woman he'd dragged back across the Atlantic to expedite a divorce!

Taking a step back, he released her and shoved his fingers through his hair, rubbing his head in rough strokes with the hope of circulating some blood to what was obviously a deprived organ. He definitely needed to run. Eight miles would be a start. Or maybe ten.

He dragged in a breath. Blew it out. "You about finished then?"

"Yes. I needed that, thank you."

Claire was gingerly arranging her skirt as she inched off the bed. Avoiding eye contact, Not that he could blame her. He'd been acting like the hound dog the rags made him out to be. Just as well she see him that way. Maybe now she'd keep her guard up instead of looking at him with those eyes that were filled with…what? It wasn't trust. It wasn't love. Hell, he had no idea what it was or what it meant except that something in the deep blue of her gaze set off something inside him he didn't like.

This woman was dangerous. More so than he'd realized before. Which was why it was imperative they get through their assets quickly. Efficiently. He'd clear meetings. Rearrange his schedule. Work twenty-three hours a day to make it happen. Whatever it took to get Claire out of his reach and out of his life once and for all. But first he had to get her a real meal and a solid night's sleep.

"Good. Then let's get you over to a hotel. Tomorrow's going to be another long day."

An hour later, Claire was booked into an ocean-view suite at the opposite end of the Shores with a cartful of room service already picked over and ready for removal. The hotel was stylish and upscale, but paled in comparison to Ryan's home-away-from-the-rest-of-his-homes. Not that it mattered. What *did* matter was she had an escape. A private sanctuary away from Ryan and the havoc he wreaked on her sanity.

She needed it.

Hands braced on the marble countertop, she stared into

the bathroom mirror searching for outward signs of her inner tumult.

None of this made sense. *It had been years*. But beginning with that moment back in Rome, it was as if her entire being surged to life, waking an awareness that had lain dormant all this time. God help her if, instead of turning away, Ryan had leaned in and kissed her, she would have let him.

Just to know for sure. If that sharp edge of arousal was real. If it could survive actual intimate contact or if it would blunt and dull. Ebb before anything could come of it.

Only, this was Ryan, and the last thing she needed were any more experiences with him.

What she needed was a means of maintaining her distance around him. Emotionally and physically.

And she had the perfect one at her very fingertips. Grabbing her phone, she spun away from the mirror and dialed the gallery.

She'd been putting work ahead of everything else in her life for years now, putting it between her and Ryan for the next week would be a breeze.

CHAPTER SIX

THIS wasn't working. The gallery was supposed to have been her buffer. Claire had instructed the on-duty manager to phone in updates throughout the day, but by lunch she'd been pulling at her scooped neckline waiting for the next call. Now the updates were coming once an hour and still it wasn't enough.

She pushed back from the dining table they'd converted to "divorce headquarters" and stretched out her neck and shoulders with a series of slow rotations. It was no good.

Ryan was everywhere. In her face. In her space. Under her skin. Leaning over the chair behind her to point out some pertinent detail about an investment property that's value tied to some other asset—and she could smell the clean spicy scent of his skin and feel the heat of his body. It was distracting and irritating and confusing and driving her insane. Twice she'd had to stop herself from snapping at him, demanding that he park himself in the far corner of the room and respect the twelve-foot space cushion she doubted would actually be enough to make her comfortable.

Because she would still *see* him.

"What is it now?"

You. Me. Us. "It's been a long day. What do you say we call it and get a fresh start in the morning?"

"Long day? Are you kidding, Claire?" A pen clattered over the tabletop behind her, followed by the scrape of a chair across the floor. "We started late so you'd be able to rest, and you've spent half your time here tied to that phone. How do you think we're going to get through all this in one week when we didn't get through one-twelfth of it today?"

"I'm sorry." She was. This was his time as well as her own and neither of them had any to waste—except she simply didn't have a choice. "But we're not going to get through it if I can't concentrate. And I can't."

He was beside her now. Frustration and concern warring in his eyes. "Are you hungry? I'll have dinner delivered. What do you want, steak, pasta?"

Holding up a hand, she warded off yet another attempt to stuff her. Bagels, cream cheese and smoked salmon had been waiting when she'd arrived. Fresh fruit and scones on offer all morning. Lunch had been burgers from the local grill down a few blocks from her hotel. And then there were the smoothies and antipasto trays brought in. She'd eaten. Plenty.

"No, thank you. All I need is another night's sleep."

It would be enough. And then she'd be back in control. Able to focus. To work. To ignore the lure of Ryan, two feet away from her.

"How 'bout we take a break instead. Get back to it in, say, ten?"

Claire cast him a doubtful look, but got distracted by the thick column of his neck and the way his open collar revealed just enough to make her want to see more.

Yeah, a break wasn't going to cut it.

Scrunching her eyes closed, she pressed a wrist to her temple where a dull ache had taken root. What was she doing? Eyeing him as if he held the key to a lock she'd thought secured forever. As if he were the key.

It was self-destructive on the basest level.

Why did it have to be him? Why after all the years of waiting for her heart and body to wake up and take a breath—did this first one have to be the long draw of Ryan Brady? And why couldn't she ignore it?

The air shifted and then he was touching her, his strong fingers sliding over the tender muscles in her neck. She froze in place, the air growing stale in her lungs as panic crept over her. "Don't."

"Aw, Claire, you've got to relax."

But how could she when he was so close the heat of his body penetrated her blouse, and his breath stirred the fine hairs behind her ears, sending chills sheeting across her skin as he muttered gruffly, "Come on, honey."

Gathering the hair at the nape of her neck into one hand, he twisted the mass and pulled it aside in a move so poignantly familiar she half believed if she were to turn around, she'd find the man she married staring down into her eyes with all the love time and fate had washed away still shining there.

What a fool she was. But not fool enough to turn and face the reality.

"No." Abruptly she tried to shove his hands away.

But just as quickly he caught her wrists, stilling her defensive efforts. "Stop."

Then slowly he pushed her resistant arms to her sides and held them steady until she gave in.

Quietly at her ear, "Just relax."

Her heart beat wildly in her chest. God, this was a mistake. He didn't know what he was doing to her—how long it had been since she'd had to contend with sensations like the ones threatening to overtake her. Making her hot. Making her ache for something beyond reach. Making her wonder if finally—

She couldn't handle it.

"Ryan," she pleaded, caught somewhere between panic and desperation.

"I know this is hard," he urged, his voice low and deep.

Understanding, though she was certain he couldn't. "I know I didn't give you any time to prepare for this—us being together. But the sooner we finish, the sooner we can move on. You get back to your life. I get back to mine. Free and clear."

His thumbs pressed firm at the base of her skull, hitting a pressure point that, as right as it was, bordered on pain. "That's what we both want, isn't it?"

"It is." She drew a long breath in through her nose and then, releasing it slowly, broke away from his hold. She didn't like being out of control. Didn't like the vulnerability. It was too much a reminder of what her life had been before. And rational or not, she resented Ryan for making her feel that way. "But a break isn't going to cut it. I'm leaving."

"What, do you have another date?" The frustration in Ryan's voice had her turning on him with a glare. She was too edgy for this.

"Don't be ridiculous, but speaking of dates, if you're so hot for company, by all means, call up yours. Or is the affair 'off again' this week?"

The corner of Ryan's mouth twisted to the side, his brows drawing down. "Why do you want to know?"

God, what was she thinking bringing Dahlia up like that? "I don't."

She didn't. Really, she didn't. Which was good, since he hadn't bothered to answer her.

"Look, I don't need your permission to leave and I'm not asking for it. As a courtesy, I'm explaining. I need to unwind."

"Right, because counting your money is so very taxing." He shoved a rough hand through his hair, shook his head and then speared her with a pointed stare. "You need to get serious about this."

Of all the nerve— "More serious than dropping my plans on a dime to accommodate a man I haven't laid eyes on in years. More serious than that, Ryan?"

If she'd been expecting him to back down or look contrite, it wasn't happening. "Damn straight. Starting with you actually sitting down with me for more than twenty-seven minutes at a stretch. Seriously, I'm stunned. Between your inability to focus and the imbeciles you've got calling every hour, I don't know how that gallery stays afloat. All hail dumb luck."

Claire's chin snapped back; her vision went red.

"Yeah, it's a real miracle I can keep the doors open, isn't it. Thank goodness I'm here with *Midas*. Do you think you could pencil in a few minutes to save me? Or are you booked on ego strokes this next week? Screw off, Ryan."

Ryan swiped at the air, knocking her snide comeback aside. "Jesus, Claire, I'm trying to help you."

Right. Leaning into his space, she glared into his eyes. "Has it ever occurred to you that I don't want your *help*? That I don't want *anything* from you at all?"

Ryan stared in blatant disbelief as her arms locked straight at her sides.

Was she serious?

His jaw ground down in a battle for restraint. A losing battle. To hell with restraint. He gave up and gave in to the hot tide of anger blistering through his veins. "Gee-whiz, Claire. Yeah, I think it may have occurred to me. A few times, in fact. Let's see, first, when you stopped talking to me. I might have gotten a clue then, and maybe another when you announced you were going back to school *half a country away*. But, gosh, honey, I think what really drove the point home for me, was *the phone call* saying you weren't coming back. Ever.

"So, yes, I have a very clear idea of what you *don't want*. But that doesn't change the fact that if I want to be free of you, I need to know I did right. That I've met my responsibilities. That you have what's yours. Only, for you to actually get it, you need my help!"

The breath beat in and out of his chest in violent draws.

What the hell was he doing yelling at her?

He needed Claire compliant. On board with his plan to knuckle down to keep working. And yet he'd drawn first blood. Delivered the low blow about the gallery when he'd known it was bull. Because he was pissed. At a situation that wasn't playing the way he'd planned. At Claire for being so damn different. At himself for about a hundred reasons starting with him being the kind of small bastard that couldn't handle it when his ex prioritized her own goals above his, and ending with his apparent inability to keep his head out of her cotton-candy-pink panties.

Damn it, he was thinking about them again—thinking about cotton candy and this new attitude Claire was wearing and how they went just right together. How they made him want to pull her into his arms and take a lick.

Only then she was leaning into him, her finger jabbing at the air with each word spat. "You want to be finished with me?"

At that moment he didn't know what the hell he wanted. Except, suddenly, clearly, he knew he wanted more of this. More of Claire's hot temper and sharp jabs. More of her fight.

"Well, news flash, Ryan, I want to be finished with you too. I want to walk away and know that my life is no one's but my own. That the only accommodations I make are on my terms. That my past is just that—in the past. I don't need your judgment. I don't want your advice. And I don't like your implication that I'm incapable of taking care of myself."

God, she was hot. Feeding his temper and making him burn. "Is that all you've got?"

He didn't have to wait for her answer to know the answer to that one.

Bring it on, beautiful.

"You want more? How about this, I'm sick of seeing your

face splashed across every rag to hit the newsstands and think-ing, 'Gee, there's my husband and his new lay! Gorgeous couple!' I *hate* being the only one who knows whether you've secretly tied the knot with your starlet—because I'm the only one who knows *you can't*! *You're still married to me*!"

She was fired up. Cheeks a hot red as she read him the riot act. Pulse hammering in the hollow against her neck. Eyes flashing challenge like a red flag in his face. She was vital. Alive. Engaged with him on a level they'd never shared before. Giving as good as she got, showing him how tough she'd become. That she wouldn't shatter if he handled her wrong.

His hands clenched at his sides. Everything about her said willful. Strong. Defiant. Everything in that moment called to him in a way he knew he ought to ignore, but just couldn't goddamn manage to.

The urge to push back rose reckless and unstoppable within him.

"That's rich, coming from Little Miss Roman Holiday," he retorted. Hey, she'd gone there first, throwing Dahlia in his face. "What was that guy's name again? Paulo, Pedro—oh, that's right. You don't know."

Claire's crystalline blues narrowed on him, sharpening focus in a way that cut straight through the part of his soul she'd once staked as her own. It shouldn't have felt good. He shouldn't have liked it. But after two days of make-nice man-ners, reined-in emotions and ironclad control, giving in to a battle of barbs with Claire was just the outlet he needed.

Based on the way she'd been coming back at him, and that gleam in her eyes, she needed it too.

"What exactly went wrong back there, Claire?" Closing in on her, he lowered his voice into a rumbling taunt. "You realize that chump couldn't give you what you wanted?"

"Go to hell."

Oh, if looks could kill, his little Claire would be looking for a no-extradition country right now. Only, she wasn't taking advantage of the chest he'd positioned within fist-hammering distance. *Yet.* "Did someone spoil you, baby?"

That did it. Her eyes went wide with shock, outrage and fury as her hand swung up to slap him. "You smug son of a—"

He caught her wrist an inch from his face, snagged the other before she could think to use it. Hell, yes. This was what he wanted. Claire, past polite. Past control. Mad enough she couldn't hide behind some mask of cool indifference. Mad enough to come at him with everything she had, let him see exactly who she'd become.

"Ah-ah," he scolded, holding both arms firm at her sides as he backed her to the wall. "It's not nice to hit."

Mad enough where that hot temper fueled more than fight in both of them.

That's what had happened. This wasn't just blowing off steam.

Not for him.

Not for her.

Claire struggled against him once, a halfhearted tug that quit almost before it began. Her eyes skirted from his mouth to his chest, lower, and then back again. Her breath came in rapid pants that pulled the gauzy fabric of her top tight with each draw.

Her nipples were hard and all he could think was the way they'd feel against his tongue.

"Let me go," she whispered.

Breaking the loose circle of his fingers, he brushed his thumb across that so-soft pulse point at her wrist.

He wanted her. But she'd told him to let her go. "Is that what you want?"

Her eyes searched his, the dark of her pupils going wide and deep. Revealing more, he was sure, than she found. All that hot aggression had shifted, exposing the tumult of emotions beneath. She was nervous. Unsure. Excited and aroused.

"I don't know," she answered, her words catching in a breathy, quiet laugh.

"Liar," he growled into the hair at the top of her head. If she'd said yes, he would have. He'd be across the room working his brain out of her panties and into the inner workings of his garbage disposal, if that's what it took.

But she hadn't. And she did know.

Claire's pulse beat in frantic rhythm with the chaos of her thoughts. This was insanity, out-and-out stupidity if she were taking any of the onus on herself. She'd been watching Ryan's every move for two days now, the heavy weight of desire building low in the pit of her belly. But she'd fought it. Shoved those hungry questions aside and tried to focus on what they were doing. Because what they were doing was working out their divorce. And because she'd thought she was the only one. But now...the tension weighing the briny sea air between them was unmistakable.

"Ryan, what is this? What are we doing?"

The fingers at her wrists skimmed outward until they threaded through hers. Slowly he drew her arms up, pinning their interlaced hands beside her head on the wall. Dark eyes roamed her features and form. Pierced the charged air vibrating between their unmet bodies.

"Giving in. To something we both want." He rocked into that empty space in a tease that hinted at contact but didn't deliver. Made her ache for it. "Something long overdue. Don't you think?"

"I can't think." Not with his big body so close that the heat of it slipped beneath her skin, turning her belly molten.

One corner of those beautiful, oh-so-very-male lips turned up, and then, as always, Ryan offered the perfect solution. "Then don't."

CHAPTER SEVEN

DON'T think.

How could she? Rational thought and conscious decision were beyond her. Annihilated by the immediate, hard press of muscle and man—familiar and foreign all at once—and the harder press of Ryan's mouth upon hers. Parting her lips beneath the crush of a kiss that was dominating and devastating and left her quivering, pinned between the wall and everything she shouldn't want.

Oh, God, how long since she'd been kissed like this, since any man had gotten close enough to kiss her at all? She'd forgotten the ecstasy of it. Of Ryan. Hot and insistent, sliding into her mouth, stroking over her teeth and tongue.

Sharing the taste and texture of his need.

So good. It was so good, she didn't want to think.

Except that wasn't how she worked anymore. It wasn't who she was.

So then what was she doing winding her arms around his neck and holding on as if she'd never let go, aching for more of that fleeting perfection she hadn't experienced in so very long, and opening wider to the kiss she shouldn't accept. All the while knowing the remnants of a marriage that never should have been lay cluttering the table behind them.

It was crazy, and yet, from the very first, she'd been weakening. Making excuses. Trying to deny the undeniable. She wanted him.

She wanted the taste of him in her mouth. The press of him over her body. She wanted what she'd thought she lost forever. She wanted it one last time. And she wanted it tonight.

One night.

Not enough time to get hurt or invest feelings that neither of them wanted or could afford.

Just long enough to set her free.

The breath she hadn't realized she'd been holding escaped in a rush. And then she was pressing into him. Arching her back so her shoulders braced the wall and her breasts rubbed his chest. Sucking at his lips and tongue, begging him for more.

His hands skimmed her waist, following the rise of her ribs until he'd covered the swells of her breasts between them, voicing his satisfaction with a deep rumble that filled her mouth.

Her hands fisted against his shirt as a needy plea escaped her. *More. Everything. Please. Now.*

Only then he stopped. His strong fingers shaped her jaw, tipping her face to the taut features of his. "Look at me, Claire. If there's even a chance you don't want this, stop me now."

She could barely breathe for wanting him so badly. There was no stopping. Not now.

He must have read the answer in her eyes though, because his mouth slammed down over hers, his tongue plunging hard and deep, retreating and driving in again. Hoisting her from her feet, he pulled her thighs to his hips, fitting them together in a way that was almost perfect, before he backed her across the room.

She couldn't get enough. Her hands were in his hair, pulling at his clothes, running over the muscles that bunched and flexed beneath the touch of her hands.

It shouldn't be Ryan. She wished it wasn't. Wished it had been any one of the decent men over the years who'd vied for her attention and walked away without success. But it wasn't.

It was Ryan. Only Ryan who held that last elusive piece to the life she so desperately needed to rebuild. That piece she'd thought lost forever.

This had to be a mistake. Deep down, Ryan knew it was. It wasn't possible to get this close to an inferno without getting burned, but the heat between them was so damn good. So hot. So out of control.

So beyond anything he'd had since before—

Don't think about it. Not now. Not like this. Not when she was blazing in his arms, over his body, and threatening to turn him inside out.

His fingers splayed wide under her spread thighs, holding her close so she rubbed against his erection with every step. She was wet.

He could feel it through the denim of his jeans and the thin fabric of those sexy pants she had on.

Ryan moved by rote until the front of his thighs hit the closest available surface. The table's edge. Divorce headquarters. Good enough.

He leaned Claire back, following her down as he swept an arm across the tabletop, clearing what had been a barely ordered mess to begin with.

They could sort it later.

Priority number one was the hellion with her legs locked around his hips, her hands jerking the buttons of his shirt free.

He had to get inside her. Had to take her.

Deep. Hot. Fast. Hard.

The primitive mantra hammered through his head as

they fought the clothing between them, rocking in restless anticipation of a union that couldn't come quickly enough.

Incoherent words of pleasure spilled from Claire's lips in needy pants, punctuated by the upward tilt of her hips, a hungry openmouthed kiss at his neck and the desperate clutch of hands, unsettled and seeking, beneath his open shirt.

"I want... Oh, God...you don't even know...so good...I need you...never thought...so long..."

A man's ego could survive an eternity on words like that alone—if his head didn't blow off first.

Fisting the gauzy fabric of a shirt that had been driving him to distraction all day, he wrenched it over Claire's head. Her hair fell in a soft tumble around her slim shoulders, neck and breasts. Dark silk and creamy skin. A barely-there lace bra in shades of nude.

His palms shaped the firm swells, taking the jutting points of her erect nipples against them as raven strands slipped and teased over the backs of his knuckles in a lure he couldn't ignore.

She was so fine. Pushing into his hands as her lips parted on a thready gasp.

Sensitive. Inviting. So damn responsive.

Echoes of her soft cries from a hundred different nights tightened his spine, demanded he test the memories against now.

Because it was different. This time it wasn't about love or forever or anything but what they simply couldn't deny a minute longer. He licked his lips and willed his brain to function. "We're just taking a time-out here."

Her legs tightened around his waist, pulling him into closer contact with all that wet heat. "A break," she panted, nodding quickly, and Ryan felt himself going harder at her eager willingness to go along. They were on the same page.

"Just two adults indulging in an adult activity." Curving

two fingers into the scant cup of her bra, he caught her nipple. Savored the sweet hitch in her breath at his gentle tug.

"And that's all?" No expectation, no demand, just the need to understand.

He held her gaze, lost himself in the depths of blue and let the truth wash over him.

"No." Even if he could lie to himself, he couldn't lie to her. "It's more than that."

"Closure." Her lips held a trace of smile as if she was only just realizing it herself.

"Closure." The idea resonated within him. The goodbye they'd never had. He rolled the tight bud, watching as her eyes smoked, her lids heavied and her head fell back, exposing the slender column of her neck. Beautiful. Wanton. Woman.

Claire.

Reaching behind him he unlocked her ankles and brought her legs around to the front, so he could strip her pants. His gaze raked hot and fast down the length of her. Lush curves and tempting hollows. And then she bowed up, squirming to unclasp her bra, pushing all that rounded, soft perfection toward him so there was no option but to lean over and take her into his mouth, close his teeth around her, and let his tongue circle the stiff tip until she cried out her broken plea, begging for more.

He yanked the last scrap of her lacy panties down the length of her legs. His hands circled her ankles and skated up her calves, catching behind her knees. Opening her to him.

Jerking at his fly with one hand, he stepped between her legs, ready—and froze.

Muttering a quiet curse, he sucked air into his lungs. Fought the tantilizing scent of her. And forced himself to meet her eyes. Eyes that were confused and hazed with heat and hurt.

"What? Please, don't stop. This will be okay, Ryan. Just now, just tonight. Just don't stop."

"No, sweetheart. Condoms, do we need them?" He didn't know how he'd gotten this far without thinking of them. Except with Claire he'd never used them. She'd been on the pill even before the first time for some regularity issues. And then she'd been—

"I won't get pregnant." If nothing else had told him how strong she'd become, the way she spoke those simple words would have. Not a flinch or flicker of the old heartbreak he knew was there. He wouldn't give her time to think about it. Not now.

"Safe sex," he answered flatly, refusing to acknowledge the pinch of discomfort he felt at voicing the necessary words. She might still be his wife, and he was relieved she had birth control taken care of, but they hadn't really been married in more than eight years. And though he'd been diligent to the extreme about protection—

"Oh, right," Claire answered, the flush across her chest and neck building darker than before, pushing into her cheeks. "Of course." She nodded quickly, then shook her head before letting out a short laugh that wasn't quite funny.

A quiet alarm began to sound from that part of him that was all instinct and gut. It wasn't guilt in her eyes. It couldn't be. They'd both had other lovers and they both knew it. So then what?

"Claire?" He brushed his thumb across the bare skin of her hip. Soothing rather than seducing. "You don't need to feel uncomfortable about this. It's not like I've been a monk."

"I know. It's just—"

"Dahlia." It had to be. "Look, the stuff in the papers isn't even close to the truth. Whatever you've read, it's not true."

Claire blinked up at him with those big blue eyes touching some part of him he didn't want to deal with. "I mean, yes, we've been together on and off. But what they say about the other women…"

"The soccer player." A woman from the U.S. Olympic team he'd been paired with…

"Before I met Dahlia. There have been a few women. Four. Two longer-term and two that were…very brief."

Damn it, this was uncomfortable. He didn't want to think about other women. He didn't want to think about anyone but Claire. And what it was going to be like when he got inside her. But to do that, he needed to do this.

"What you said before about me being 'off again' with Dahlia, it's just off. For over a month now. And for the record, I use condoms every time."

If he'd been expecting the tension to be wiped from Claire's face at hearing he wasn't half the player the rags made him out to be, it didn't happen. If anything, she looked more uncomfortable.

And then quietly she asked, "Are you waiting for me to tell you…my sexu—"

"No," he choked out as jealousy snagged unexpectedly in his throat. He shut his eyes, trying to blot out the images that too quickly filled his mind. That was the last damn thing he wanted to hear.

"I know there've been other men." All he needed to know now was whether he was going to have to beat the world speed record in a sprint to the market down on Avenida de la Playa or whether he took her hilt deep *now*.

Only, then he caught her expression—and the world around them ground to a halt.

Hell, he knew that face. The one that tried to hide the truth stamped so blatantly across it. She turned away with an awkward shift, averting her gaze. The woman who'd been bare and open to him without a second's hesitation didn't want him to see her eyes.

Catching her chin in his hand, he brought her face back to his. "There *have* been other men."

The wince was almost imperceptible. Anyone who wasn't looking for it—praying it wouldn't come—would have missed it. But it was there.

No. He *couldn't* be right about this.

Let his blasted gut and instinct have turned worthless overnight.

"Please," she begged, trying to pull back from his grasp.

She couldn't do this to him. Panic crawled up this neck as unwilling certainty settled over him.

"Tell me I'm wrong! Tell me there's been someone else."

Just the one! he silently roared. Give him something. Anything. But as her gaze held with his, he knew.

"Ryan—"

"No." He jerked the clothes hanging half off his body back into place as memories of the past years accosted him with sickening force. He'd moved on...because she had. There hadn't been any guilt. But now.

All this time. How could she—

He nearly choked. "Have you been waiting for me to come after you?"

"God, no!" It was worse than Claire could have imagined.

She reached for him, only to have her hand pressed away.

"Then what?" he demanded, anguish and accusation warring in his eyes. "How?"

The sincerity of the question, one she couldn't believe he wouldn't understand, sliced through her concern and compassion, exposing the old hurt she'd tried so hard to overcome.

"*How?* How can you even ask? You were there. You saw me. What I was like. After we lost Andrew—" Images of his too-tiny body assaulted her, constricting her chest. Shaking her head, she forced air in and out of her lungs, refusing to give in to the dark emotions that threatened to swamp her when she delved too deeply into the old pain. "I was broken. To my soul."

"I know you were...different." He crossed to her, grabbing her arms and then setting her back from him as though to touch her was both necessity and beyond tolerable. "I took you to counseling. Yes, I knew. But all this time? I thought—I *believed* you'd—"

He jerked away from her, shoving his fingers through his hair as agony shone in his eyes. "Damn it, Claire, I *saw* another man leaving your apartment! Five in the morning. What the hell was that?"

CHAPTER EIGHT

HE'D *seen* her. And, while nearly killing him, it had been the key to his sanity. The free pass he'd taken and run with. Claire had moved on. Taken that irrevocable step and given up on the marriage they'd stopped fighting for years before.

He'd been sickened and relieved all at once. Reluctant and determined that night when he'd gone out and found a woman—one who wasn't looking for anything more than he was.

It hadn't been beautiful or meaningful or intense. It had been an act. An escape. One he'd hated himself for taking. But after that he'd been free.

And he'd refused to look back.

Only now, the confusion painted across Claire's face had him twisting with denial, scouring the gritty details of a memory he'd tried to forget.

"What are you talking about?" she demanded, taking the clothes he'd so recently stripped her of and pulling them on in jerky movements.

He wanted to help. To reach out and straighten the sleeve that had somehow turned around and inside itself. But, God help him, he couldn't touch her right then. Couldn't stand the feel of his own damn skin as the framework of who he was, the choices he made, and how he lived began to crumble around him.

"Back in New York. I went to your apartment. You were finished with school. You'd told me you weren't coming back." His teeth ground down as he dragged a breath through his nose. "I'd flown in on the red-eye. And when I got to your place, I saw him. Saw you walk him out to the front stoop. Put your arms around his neck." Had he known she hadn't slept with him—

What would it have mattered?

Even if she hadn't been interested in another man, she hadn't been interested in him either. He would have been waiting around like a fool for something that would never have happened.

An old knife twisted through his gut, making him push back and cross to the far corner of the room before she could see the reaction he didn't want to acknowledge to himself, let alone her.

New York. Claire remembered. She knew whom he was talking about. Only one man had spent the night with her since she'd left Ryan. But he'd slept on the couch, not in her bed, and sex had been the last thing between them.

God, to think he'd flown through the night to see her and instead saw that. If only she'd known he'd been there, she could have explained. Saved him the hurt or betrayal or whatever it was he'd felt.

No. There weren't any if onlys. She'd stopped playing that game a long time ago.

"That was Joe Nevin. He was a good friend, and he did spend the night. Only, we didn't...." Her words trailed off. She couldn't say it. "He'd lost his wife. It was the anniversary of her death and he needed a friend. He drank too much and I let him stay on the couch. But even if the circumstances had been different, I wouldn't have been able to spend the night with him the way you're talking about."

Ryan caught her reflection in the glass. "Because of me?"

"Not you. Me." Partly because her body hadn't physically recovered from the trauma that put her back in the emergency room the week before—one she hadn't told Ryan about then and wouldn't burden him with now. Especially not now.

But that was only half the reason.

Claire wrapped her arms around herself, refusing to think about how warm she'd been in Ryan's arms just a few minutes before.

All that was gone now.

"What happened between us. The way things changed after I lost our baby. The way I stopped responding to you... It was everything, Ryan. I didn't feel. I didn't care. I barely existed. It was as if my entire world went gray." She straightened her shoulders. "I've been working for a long time to get back to *living* rather than just existing. And mostly I've done it. But in some ways..." She drew a slow breath, held her hands out helplessly before her.

"Only, then you showed up and, I don't know how or why, but suddenly it's like a switch flipped. *You make me feel.* And I wanted that. I thought you'd take me to bed and I'd finally have all the pieces of myself I'd lost, back again." It wasn't the whole truth. She knew she couldn't be put back together the same way she once was, that there were parts of who she'd been that were lost forever. But of those that were salvageable, this was the last one.

"You weren't going to tell me."

"No." If she'd been able to keep that secret, Ryan never would have known. It exposed a part of her she didn't want shared. Worse yet, she recognized the toll this truth had taken on him. It was written in the lines of his face. Ryan didn't take his responsibilities or commitments lightly. He'd married her because she was pregnant and he would have stayed with her through those dark times no matter what it cost him...if she'd let him. He wouldn't have left because that was the kind of man he was.

That day in New York she'd unknowingly given Ryan the permission he'd needed to move on. And now he'd just found out everything he believed was wrong.

She reached out to him, only to drop her hands at the last second. Better she just leave. Quietly she gathered her bag, surveying the devastation they'd left in their wake.

Folders and reports were strewn across the floor and only a single leaf of paper remained atop the table that had once been nearly covered. "I thought we could give each other a last night together, something good. But I see that all I've done is take something away. I'm sorry, Ryan. I didn't mean to."

Moments after watching Claire collect herself and leave, Ryan shoved through to the master suite, only vaguely registering the door bouncing shut behind him. Blindly he stalked the length of his floor and back, straining for control as adrenaline and testosterone, mixing at toxic levels, beat a violent path through his veins. Hammered past his ears in a deafening roar.

Six years, he'd been completely, perfectly, contentedly ignorant. Wielding that damn image of a man leaving her place like a weapon every time guilt tried to gnaw at the comfort of the life he'd built.

He hadn't been the one to give up. That's what he told himself. He hadn't quit first. Because that wasn't the kind of man he was, it wasn't how he'd been raised. He may not have had a man at home to teach him about being a father or husband, how to *be there* for a wife who needed him, but he understood commitment and responsibility.

Only, he'd been wrong.

He hated that. Hated himself and hated Claire for disrupting the reality he'd so easily accepted. For making him wonder. Doubt. For giving him one more failure to heap on the pile building since nearly the day he'd first met her.

Why hadn't he just gotten out of that damn car? Walked up to her door and confronted her. She would have told him the truth, and they could have gone forward from there.

Not together. Even then it had already been too late. Their marriage had died years before. There was no resuscitating it.

That part of the story wouldn't change no matter what he'd known or when.

But if he'd manned up and talked to her—instead of letting the months slip past, turn into years—they would have had to face facts. It was over. They could have ended it then.

And now Claire would be nothing more than a distant memory.

Right. Because she was so easy to forget.

Hell, he could still taste her skin on his tongue. Smell her hair in his clothes. Feel her burning beneath his hands, against his chest...around his hips. His fists clenched at his sides. She'd been ready. Hot and wet and so damn eager.

Desperate. For him.

Because in nine years she hadn't had another man.

Why did it have to affect him so much? Knowing he'd been the only one. That on some primitive level he hadn't wanted to acknowledge, *she was still his.*

His hand sliced through the air in aimless aggression.

He didn't need this. It wasn't what he'd planned or expected. But then nothing was going the way he expected with Claire. That truth had been bombarding him since the first minute he laid eyes on her in Rome. He'd wanted her then, even if he hadn't wanted to admit it—because he'd known it would be a mistake.

Except it didn't feel like a mistake. Not when she'd been burning like wildfire beneath his touch, and, damn it, not when she told him he was the only one. The only thing that felt wrong had been the one thing he should have been used to by now. Watching her go.

Claire paced the winding pebble path of Ryan's interior garden, waiting for her cab to arrive. A tremble ran through her and, wrapping her arms around her middle, she sank onto the driftwood chaise. The garden, like everything else in the house, was a masterpiece of balance between contrasts and complements. Colors, textures and scents. Time, motion and light. Young bamboo shoots, hip height, slender and vivid green, rustled in the night breeze opposite a twelve foot sculptural installation of petrified bridge supports preserved from a river in China. Brightly colored birds of paradise craned above chubby-leaved ground cover. And cocoa husks buried beneath the varied foliage and brush infused the otherwise briny sea air with the rich scent of decadent comfort.

A comfort Claire couldn't embrace.

What a disaster. The last thing she'd wanted to do was add to the guilt and responsibility Ryan already carried on his shoulders because of her. But that's what had happened tonight. And now, so much damage had been done she couldn't fathom a counter to it.

Tomorrow she'd have to return. She'd have to face Ryan knowing how close they'd come to making love. And how everything had gone to hell because of it.

A horn honked twice. Her cab.

Pushing up from the bench, she walked to the gate. "I'm coming."

Only, after a dumbfounding moment, she realized she had no idea how to open it. Every time she'd come or gone, it had been through the side driveway with an electric gate she didn't know how to access. This exit was a six-foot-wide square that had once been a Buddhist temple ceiling. Elaborately carved in an intricate floral relief, the smoke-blackened panel was stunning and stupefying all at once.

She pulled at the handle. It didn't budge. Searched in vain for a latch and felt her face heating at the notion of having to seek out Ryan just so she could leave his house. No. There had to be a way.

"One more minute, please," she called to the waiting cab, going up on tiptoe to feel for a release or catch. Nothing.

"Like this." The deep murmur came from startlingly close behind, and Claire jumped as Ryan reached around her to push a recessed button while simultaneously pulling the handle. The gate swung soundlessly open, forcing her to step back into the heat of his body. But already he was moving around her, his eyes holding briefly with hers.

"We're not done."

Ryan jogged to the waiting cab and handed off a few bills through the open window with an apology for the inconvenience.

And then he was back. A dark silhouette amid the shadows, Ryan was unreadable in his features, but radiated a tension that was unmistakable nonetheless. Intimidating.

He closed the gate behind him. Preventing her exit with his presence more than his physical form.

"I drove you over here. I can take you back. Later."

Pressing her lips together, she nodded. After what happened, or nearly happened, she supposed they should talk. Clear the air, if only to agree to leave the incident behind them. Now more than ever they needed to be able to work through the division of the assets as a team. Finish the job quickly. Finish everything.

"I'm sorry," she began, then let her gaze drift as she tried to pinpoint from where exactly the remorse welling inside her originated. It was there, a tide of regret, but for what? What might have been? Hurting Ryan? She didn't even know.

The silence stretched taut until the rough edge of Ryan's voice cut through it. "Are you still broken, Claire?"

"What?" She jolted at the unexpected direction of his inquiry, wondered if he'd somehow figured out what had happened. If he knew—

"Your soul. Your heart. I look at you and I almost see the woman I married. But you're not. I don't know you the way I knew her. You look strong. Alive. Whole. But I don't know... So I have to ask. Are you still broken?"

Her heart rattled, unsteady in her chest.

"No..." Her life was nearly what she'd hoped for it. And yet, at times... "Not the way I was."

"That guy in Rome," he asked. "Did he make you feel... anything?"

She closed her eyes, thinking back. Everything had happened so quickly, she hadn't really had time to ponder her response before Ryan's name alone had killed the chance for anything more. At first it had been enough to know the man's touch hadn't repelled her. She'd been aware of it on a superficial level, aware that it might have been nice, but not connected closely enough to the experience, to the man...

"No." She swallowed. "But I wanted it to."

She couldn't be sure beneath the thick shadows, but she thought she saw a muscle jump in his jaw. "Because you found him attractive."

"Because I wanted to be *normal*. I wanted to have my life back. I wanted a chance—" Her throat constricted tight around the emotion tinged with hopes and dreams she told herself not to imagine.

"And with me?" he asked, stepping closer and drawing her out of her quiet turmoil. Breaching the moonlight, the hard set of his jaw and taut lines of his face stood out in sharp relief. "You *feel* when you're with me?"

This wasn't cocky arrogance or ego speaking. It was the

man she trusted above all others asking her for a truth he deserved to have. "I don't want to."

Because she didn't want Ryan to be the answer to another one of her problems. Didn't want to put another obligation out in front of the man who met them as though it was a compulsion.

His lips slanted into a wry twist. "But that's not what I asked."

Forcing her chin up, she met his eyes. "Yes."

He moved into the space she occupied. The flex of his fingers at his side set her every sense on wild alert. This was worse than she could have imagined. The one thing she wanted—the one way she couldn't live with having it.

"I know you want to feel complete again, and you see this as the last step to getting there. But I need you to understand something, Claire."

She shivered beneath the heat of his breath washing over the column of her neck. Aching with a need she couldn't sate.

"I'm not here to help you heal so you can learn to be with some other man. I'm not selfless—" his lips grazed her collarbone "—and I'm not heroic. I'm here because I want you so bad, the idea of not having you kills me. But there's only one way this is happening, and that's if *you* want *me*."

Her breath burst free in unburdened relief. Ryan was wrong. He was all those things. Just not, thank God, tonight. There was no doubt, no hesitation or second-guessing. Nothing but a trembling desperation. "I want you."

CHAPTER NINE

CLAIRE had barely the span of a second for her breath to catch before the kiss blotted out all but the rough press of his lips covering hers. There was no question, no testing measure of restraint, and her acceptance was scored in the willing give of her mouth as she opened beneath the demand of his lips. Moaned around the claim of his tongue and reveled in the tightening band of the arms holding her to him.

Ryan knew the truth and still he'd come back.

His mouth slid over hers, hot and hungry.

He'd come back because *he wanted her as badly as she wanted him*. Not because of some misplaced sense of guilt or obligation. But because of mutual attraction.

Liquid heat sizzled through her veins, slid through her center and sensitized her flesh. Her mind blanked to all but the seductive experience, making her fingers tingle and twinge with the need for contact.

Shared breath passed between their lips in intimate exchange. A swirling caress of warm and wet, drawing deep until it filled and stretched the empty hollows within. Lingered. Then escaped, only to be taken by the other. After so many years without intimacy, Claire shuddered at the base sensuality of it. Felt her womb tightening with the need for more.

The need for Ryan.

She wanted him. Wanted his strength and desire penetrating her completely, infusing every cell of her being.

Her hands moved desperately between them, climbing the fabric of his shirt, clutching at his shoulders, his neck, then delving into the thick silk of his hair.

He broke away from her lips only to work his way down her jaw to the tender skin beneath. A scrape of teeth shot lightning through her core and she moaned at the sensation. Was stunned by her body's near betrayal in its utter surrender after all the years of refusal to stir.

"Do you have any idea," Ryan growled against her throat, the vibration of his voice sending chills skittering across her skin, "what a mistake it would have been not to tell me how long it's been for you?"

Eyes pinched shut, she didn't want to think about it. Didn't want him to, either. "Ryan, I'm sorry."

"You would have been." His tongue ran the length of the tendon in her neck in a deliberate, slow, back-and-forth caress that had her hips seeking his.

The hot burst of his breath rushed across the cool damp trail he'd laid and she groaned beneath the sensual wash.

"You don't understand." His hold tightened as a muttered curse ground out against her pulse point. "The way you respond to me…I wouldn't have held back. I wouldn't have known to. And the way I want you…"

Another low growl behind her ear. "I had you on the table. Open to me."

Her heart stalled and her skin pebbled from tip to toe.

"It wouldn't have been gentle, Claire." His voice deepened, the words coming like a rough-tongued caress against the most sensitive parts of her body. "It wouldn't have been slow."

A pleading moan escaped on her next breath as seductive images bombarded her mind, Ryan over her, thrusting

gave herself over to his command. Her weight shifted and she allowed him to guide her leg to notch at his hip.

And then his fingers were slipping through her, back and forth, holding contact with that bit of flesh that made her writhe for him. Pant. Plead.

He brought his mouth back to hers, parting her lips with the press of his tongue, and pushed a single finger inside her. She was wet and hot and tight. And God, yes, those silky walls were clasping around him in rhythmic strains as he slid in and out of her, stroking deep until she was so close he could feel her body bow taut against him. Her breath stopped as she hovered at the brink. Ready to come apart for him.

In and out. She hugged him tighter.

"Oh, God. Ryan. Please..."

The slam of a car door and muted chatter of a couple beyond the gate ripped him back from the haze of seduction, had his head jerking up as he silently cursed his poor choice of location.

He hadn't been able to wait to touch her.

"Don't stop...I can't..." She shook her head, her whispered pleas washing his neck with her need, making it his own.

Claire's body pulsed with desire nearly fulfilled. Her heart raced and her breath held. She was so close. Already there. Caught in the force of a wave where the crash was imminent.

"Breathe, kitten," he growled against her lips.

Ryan's erection nudged hard and thick at her hip, his lips brushing hers as he thrust inside her, first with one thick finger, and then stretching her to take two.

She gasped at the straining pressure. Spasmed around the next thrust as sparks of wild hot sensation shot across her skin, drew back, deepened, built, centered. Pulsed hard and pushed her over the edge in an explosion of white-hot pleasure.

"Shh. I've got you." His mouth covered hers, catching the

low keening cry she couldn't contain as the world around her went up in flames, turning her body to cinders.

Catching in the wind, she spiraled skyward. Light. Soft. She was finally free.

CHAPTER TEN

THEY'D made it halfway up the first flight before giving in to greedy hands and mouths left them in a tangle of writhing limbs atop the steps. Claire's legs cinched at his hips, her arms rounded his neck as Ryan devoured her mouth with a hunger that left her breathless.

He'd given her release. Set her free only minutes before, but it wasn't enough. She wanted more. Wanted all of him. Wanted everything again, and again after that—just to make sure it was real.

With the strength of one arm, Ryan rocked her against the steely shaft of his erection. One touch and he had her hooked, desperate for the drug only he could deliver.

"Shirt," she urged, aching for his bare flesh beneath her fingers.

Rearing back, he grabbed a handful of the fabric between his shoulders and wrenched it overhead. Lightning lanced her core as bunched muscles ripped free above her and the hard cut expanse of his bared torso was once again within reach.

God only knew how long she'd have this. An hour. A night at the most. Unwilling to waste even a second, she bowed into him, letting her tongue run between the hard ridges of his six-pack, her teeth graze the tops.

Ryan's breath sucked in on a hiss. "Claire, I need to get inside you."

Her shirt was yanked off, followed immediately by her pants, both stripped by hands too impatient to wait for her to do it herself. And then she was naked except for her delicately beaded sandals with their slim high heels and open toes.

"Upstairs. Bed." Hauling her into his bare chest, he rose, took the steps two at a time until they hit the third floor. Rounding the corner, he shouldered them through the door and reached out for the wall switch, dropping them into darkness.

Unlocking her ankles from where they tucked against the low hang of worn denim riding his hips, Claire slid to stand before him.

"I don't want slow, Ryan." Her hands rushed over the hard planes of his chest, setting the muscles beneath to jump at her touch. Then drifted lower until she'd skimmed beneath his fly. Palming his hardness, she wrapped her fingers over the length of him.

"Claire." Her name sounded in a low growl, rolling in like a warning. A warning she couldn't bear to heed.

"And I don't want gentle."

He already knew. She could see it in his eyes, feel it in the firming hold of his hands at her hips. Sense it on the currents charging the air.

Brushing her hands aside, Ryan shucked his pants and drew her hard against him. Backed her across the room.

And then he was pressing her into the mattress and following her down. Kneeing her thighs apart and holding her gaze as he notched himself against her. "What do you want, Claire?"

For one fleeting second, time touched back upon itself and Ryan was the man poised to take her virginity.

That night, he'd held himself in relentless check, working himself into the snug hold of her body with infinite care and patience, using his every sensual skill to bring her to climax even as he breached her fragile barrier.

She'd given him her body those years ago, and now, tonight, he gave it back.

"You. I want to feel you inside me." She met his eyes and slid her fingers over the taut skin of his chest. "Please."

He thrust—not with the slamming force she'd imagined, thought she'd wanted—but with a steady, driving pressure. Inch by inch he pushed inside her, forcing her awareness of his growing claim through the sensual onslaught of each nerve bursting to frenzied life.

It was too much. Too good. More than she could bear and everything she wanted.

"Can you feel me, Claire?" he demanded through gritted teeth, the sound of his voice rough like gravel, as the head of his penis nudged her womb and his groin met the kiss of her feminine flesh.

"Yes." Like the first time, it hurt. The sheer size of him, even after he'd prepared her, stretched with a pressure that left her torn between begging him to stop and pleading for more. And like the first time, he filled her with something beyond the physical. Made her wonder at how she'd managed to go so long without.

"Tell me," he growled against her ear, angling his hips to penetrate deeper.

"Yes," she cried out again. "I feel you." So good. So deep, she seized around him, her inner muscles clamping down against the blessed strain.

A harsh curse sounded at her ear and he drew back, the wet friction spurring her oversensitive nerves to scream in rioting pleasure even as her lips parted on a soundless gasp. Another full-length thrust, another shattering response, another retreat and then all of it again. Harder.

Not slow. Not gentle.

Ryan's jaw clenched as he held fast to the restraint threatening to snap under the agonizing pleasure of each movement. She was so tight. So hot and wet and good around him that forgetting he'd been the only one was impossible. With each torturous thrust into the snug hold of her, with every hilt-deep plunge, every mind-blowing grip of her body winding impossibly tighter around his, he felt it.

She was his.

He didn't want to acknowledge it. Didn't want to revel in it. But the claim was there.

Mine.

In every moan of pleasure. Every shuttle in and out of her slick grasp.

Mine.

No one had touched her.

Mine.

No one had stirred her to want.

Mine.

Every sound she made. *Belonged to him.*

It was insanity. And she'd brought him there as easily as she had nine years before.

Mine. Mine. Mine.

He pumped faster, groaning at the clingy grasp of her inner walls. Angled deeper. Thrust harder, until her body pulsed with need, her thighs clutching at his hips even as her fingers dug into his shoulders. It was so good, too good, and then she was coming around him, her neck craning back, her lips parting in gasping, breathless pleasure, until at last she managed a single word.

"Ryan."

And tumbled over the edge.

Beautiful. She was breathtaking in her release. And as fired as his blood was to give in—more, he wanted to savor this moment. Synch his stroke with the waves of her climax and draw it out. Watch her as she came apart and forged together anew.

For him. Only him.

Her breath steadied, eased. And then beneath the pale wash of starlight that spilled through the unshaded windows, he saw the tears streaming from her eyes.

"Ah, Claire," he whispered, shifting to his elbows to brush the glittering moisture from her temples. "Don't regret this."

Blinking up at him, she ran her hands over his jaw with that butterfly touch and shook her head. "I don't. I couldn't."

"Then what are the tears?"

A tremulous smile touched her lips, a fragile thing that made his response to it all the more powerful.

"Relief. Joy... Freedom maybe?" She swallowed, holding his gaze, revealing her emotions in a way that knocked the breath from his chest. "What you've given back to me tonight...I thought I'd lost forever."

After taking so many things he could never return, it was about time he'd found something he could give back. Something that meant more to her than half the damn fortune he'd amassed and she couldn't seem to care less about.

How was it she could still make his heart beat like this? Make him feel like a king rather than a thief, when all the evidence to the contrary was scattered in the years behind them.

"You can't understand what it means to me."

Looking down into her eyes and seeing the trust, the joy, feeling her body respond around his. Knowing that in this moment, she was truly happy, he understood, more than she could imagine.

Claire's knees skimmed higher on his hips, her fingers drifting across his shoulders. She arched a brow at him, teasing and pure Claire. "You aren't done."

"No." Targeting those lush lips of hers for a quick nip, he began to move his hips with renewed purpose. "And neither are you."

Claire stood at the terrace door and watched the ocean roll and churn, spitting froth against the midnight sky. She'd woken a half hour before—heart racing, mind instantly alert, body... alive. Unable to return to sleep and too restless to lie still, she'd slipped from the warm hold of Ryan's arms and fumbled through the semidarkness until she'd found something to pull on. One of Ryan's enormous suit shirts, it turned out. The fine cotton caressed her from shoulder to thigh, teasing her sensitive skin in a luxurious reminder of what they'd done. Of what Ryan had given her. And how pure that gift had been. What they'd done had been about pleasure. Not debt or obligation or responsibility or any of the other too heavy burdens that had been so much a part of their past together.

She shook her head wishing she had the words to make him understand how this single night had changed everything for her. But how could he? He'd been living a life that was whole from the start. Or the end. Whatever it was to him when they split up. But she hadn't. No matter how far she'd come, no matter what she accomplished building her career, her life, there had been this glaring hole in the middle of her existence—a dark void that prevented anyone from getting too close.

And now the kind of life she hadn't even dared to dream of was within her grasp. There were still limits on what she had to offer, but she wasn't irrevocably broken. She wasn't missing that singular piece of herself that she could never ask a man to live without. She could move on. Finally let someone else in.

Though even as she thought it, she found herself glancing

over her shoulder at the sleeping man behind her, resisting the ache that built in the depths of her chest.

She couldn't afford to give in to that ache.

This time they had together was, after all, about closing the door to a long overdrawn chapter of their lives. Even making love—especially making love—was about moving on. Ending their marriage with a bit of the beauty it began with.

But tonight she still had Ryan.

Crossing to the bed, she slipped out of the shirt, wanting only the skin on bare skin between them. The mattress shifted beneath her as she kept an eye on Ryan's sleeping form. There'd been a time when her return to bed would have had him reaching for her in his sleep.

Not tonight.

Silly. That twinge of disappointment.

Pulling a corner of the sheet to cover her, she laid her head on the pillow—and felt the heavy pull of Ryan's powerful arm wrap around her, drawing her into the hold of his body.

A slow sigh escaped her lips and she closed her eyes amid the sensation of warmth and intimacy.

Half asleep, he probably wasn't even aware of who she was beyond a female body in his bed. But it didn't matter. She knew who he was, and the heat of his arms surrounding her felt so good, she'd take it.

And then, as she drifted down into the bliss of oblivion where even the wildest, most forbidden dreams could be realized, a breath teased through her hair…carrying the sleep-thickened murmur of her name.

CHAPTER ELEVEN

RYAN woke to the faint glow of purple leaching night from the sky as dawn readied to break.

He'd slept with his wife.

Slept! As if the actual sex hadn't been bad enough, he'd pulled her into his arms. Taken the sweet curve of her body against his own and let go.

Sure. Just a couple of minutes to catch his breath. Soothe any anxieties or fears Claire might have had. The last thing she'd need after nearly a decade of celibacy would be the first man she gave it up to, to hop out of bed with a wink and salute. *"Thanks for the great time, babe. You were dynamite."*

He'd *had* to stay a while.

Yeah, right.

Except then she'd gone lax in his arms, her breath falling into the quiet rhythm of sleep, and still he'd held her. Let his mouth rest against the slope of her shoulder, his nose bury into the silky sheets of her hair. His arm band across her so the soft puffs of her breath whispered over his knuckles where they rested at her pillow.

Of all the damn fool things to do, falling asleep like that topped the list.

As if the years apart, years of lost dreams, separate lives, different cities, different women, for God's sake!—as if none of it had happened.

And why?

Because he'd made her *want*…made her *come*…because he'd given her something she'd been missing, and the look in her eyes had made him feel like a god?

What a laugh.

He had to get out of there.

Gently disentangling himself from the intimate embrace of Claire's limbs, he was ready to roll away, when her sultry purr stopped him short. That sound. Damn if it didn't get under his skin…slip into his veins and ride a hot trail of possession through the very heart of him.

"Where you going?" came the groggy inquiry.

Break's over, kitten. That's what he should say. Call it one night. Kiss her long and slow, sweet and tender. Give them both a nice pretty bow to wrap around the remnants of a marriage they'd agreed more than once never should have been, while sending a nice clear message about distance and expectation.

Except he couldn't say a word. Couldn't do anything but follow the contours of her body beneath his sheets and think this *was* where she belonged.

In his bed.

The disturbing reality settled around him. Now that he'd had her, he wouldn't be able to leave her alone. As long as that sleek fall of black hair was within reach, he'd be wrapping it around his fist to pull her closer.

Which didn't mean they'd suddenly be calling off the divorce. Hell, no. This wasn't some kind of second chance at the wildfire that had nearly destroyed them the first time. This, now, was a controlled burn. The very ashes of their past together serving as the limit on its destructive potential. Because fire couldn't feed on what no longer existed, and all those old expectations, emotions and youth-fueled fantasies were gone now. For both of them.

Ryan leaned on one arm, looking down at Claire half asleep beneath him. He stroked a few dark strands from her face, and then trailed the tip of his finger across the rise of her cheekbone, into the soft divot behind her ear, and then lower to the swell of her breast. Tracing slow circles around the shell-pink areola, he watched her nipple bead tight beneath his touch. Her breath hitch and stall. The dark fringe of her lashes flutter open to reveal sleep-heavy eyes, already hazed with arousal.

Her lips parted for the wet tip of her tongue and Ryan's groin hardened to the point of pain.

"One more time?" she murmured, her knee sliding against his thigh in silky-soft invitation.

Another revolution around the berry-hard tip, teasingly close, but not yet closing in. "Is that all you want? One more time?"

"What are you asking?"

Lowering his head, he took her into his mouth and tested her ripeness against the curl of his tongue. The sinuous arch of Claire's back and press of her breast, coupled with her soft cry, was satisfying surrender. His fingers skimmed low over her belly and into the notch between her legs where she was warm and snug.

"Until the divorce is finalized, Claire." Gently he pushed a finger inside her, watched as her eyes glazed even as she struggled for clarity. He stroked into her. Groaned at the tight hug as she spasmed around his intrusion. Slipped his hand free and painted her moisture around her opening. "No expectations beyond that."

"We'd have a week." Her thighs fell farther apart, opening her to him completely.

Ryan shifted so his knees were between her legs, his shaft nudging at the entrance to her body. Slowly, he pushed home.

"Not enough," he said through clenched teeth, bowing his

head against the mind-blowing pleasure of their fit, pulling out as far as he dared, and then pushing back in deep.

Claire cried out, clutching at his shoulders as her heels sought purchase on the backs of his thighs. "How long?"

He thrust again, rotating his hips before pulling back and then doing it again.

How long could he have her—have this—without someone getting hurt? A week wasn't going to be enough. He knew it without a doubt. With a limit of five more days, the only time he'd let her out of bed would be to take her in the shower. Or on the table. The floor. The ocean. The beach. Beneath the sheared-off cliffs at the tide pools.

If all he had was a week, he wouldn't let Claire even get close to divorce headquarters. And he took his commitment to secure her future too seriously for that. They needed more time to let this run its course.

"As long as it takes." Thrusting again, he stilled, buried deep inside her. Her sea-blue eyes stared up at him as he rocked his groin against her pelvic bone, catching her clitoris between them. She seized around him, sucking in her breath on a gasp as she pulled her knees higher against his ribs.

Oh, yeah, she liked that.

"We'll work around our schedules." He rocked again. "Meet weekends when we can." Ducking down for a kiss, he thrust his tongue in sync with his hips for a single deep taste. Then, "Go through the assets one by one."

"It makes sense," she half moaned, rising beneath him to match his every stroke. "We wouldn't have to rush."

"No rush," he agreed, rocking against her again. Her fingers wound into his hair, holding him tight as she strained upward, begging for more. She was close.

"We'd have time to be thorough." Her breath was coming in thready gasps now. The color high across her cheeks and chest.

"Meticulous, Claire." Another hilt-deep thrust. Another spasm. Another slow grinding rock of his body against hers and she broke. Came apart around him, crying out his name as he followed her into bliss.

Moments later, still buried inside her, he rolled to his side, bringing Claire with him. "We both know what this is. Just like we both know what it isn't."

"Temporary. An affair."

An affair with his wife. Crazy, but accurate. "And when it's over—"

Her fingers smoothed over his lips, following the contours in a seductive study that had him stirring where he was still connected to her body. How was it like this with her?

Claire's gaze met his, a soft smile playing at her mouth. "When it's over we go our separate ways, leave the past behind, and take something beautiful away with us."

And then the blaze between them would simply burn itself out.

No expectations beyond that. No one hurt.

That was the biggest thing. In his life, there'd been nothing worse than the impotent rage he'd experienced watching her suffer. Knowing, ultimately, he'd been at the root of it, but that nothing he did could make it better. He'd gotten her pregnant and she'd lost her parents over it. And then she'd lost the baby and all she'd had left was him. A twenty-two-year-old jackass who'd thought he knew how to be a husband, but didn't have a clue. Nothing he'd done was right. Nothing helped.

He wouldn't go through that again. No matter how badly he wanted her.

But they weren't shooting for forever here or looking to build something lasting or solid. Claire didn't need that kind of shelter. She'd healed and was stronger than she'd ever been before. She knew what they were getting into and she wanted it. Their cards were laid plainly on the table. What you see is what you get. No surprises. No opportunity for heartbreak.

Safe in that knowledge, Ryan reached for Claire's hip and, groaning against the rising need between them, he took her again.

CHAPTER TWELVE

Snow was falling outside her window. Bits of downy chill chasing through the New York night air in what seemed a shocking contrast to the California sunshine Claire had left behind that morning.

Pulling the thick terry of her robe around her, she turned from the window and crossed back to the couch, dropping into the overstuffed cushions as Sally's outraged voice spilled across the miles and into her ear.

"You never make this kind of bad decision, Claire. What were you thinking?"

What indeed. Only then she realized, for the first time in five minutes Sally had stopped talking and a response was expected at that point.

There was only one thing she could say.

"I wanted him. I know that sounds crazy, but I honestly couldn't stop myself. I didn't even want to." Tucking her feet beneath her, she snuggled back into the corner and sighed. "It was like there was something unfinished between us—"

"And now it's done? Now the reasonable woman I know and love like she was my very own blood has returned, ousting the sex-crazed imposter who took over her body these last days. Is that right?"

"Not exactly." She could still hear him, above her. *"Not enough."* That guttural admission that had set her on fire and, even now, made her heat in ways that wouldn't be satisfied until they met again.

"How, exactly, do you mean *not exactly*?" Sally demanded, making Claire want to laugh at this impatient show of protection. It had always been the other way around with them. Sally was the vulnerable one. The little sister of her heart, the impetuous girl that Claire protected. It had been that way since she'd found her five years ago outside the gallery. Lost and left behind by a boyfriend who had promised her the world and brought her to New York, only to abandon her with less than seventeen dollars when he met someone who "got him and his vision." Claire had taken her in. Given her a job and helped her with school. And Sally had given her everything she had in return. They were more like sisters than friends or employer and employee. And Claire had always been the big sister...but today, the roles had reversed.

A part of her wondered if the change had anything to do with Massimo, the man Sally had stayed behind to be with... and now stubbornly refused to discuss, brushing all questions aside with a flat "we're not talking about me". Not that the same line had done a thing for Claire. Sally wasn't having any of it.

She didn't know how to explain the pull she felt toward Ryan. Didn't want to explain what she'd never admitted to Sally or anyone but Ryan before—that there had been no one else. That until him, she hadn't even felt the flicker of a spark toward another man. "It's different with Ryan. Sally, the way we ended things—there's so much unresolved between us."

Ryan had been everything to her. The rising sun, laughter beneath the midday rays, and love through the star-speckled nights. But after Andrew...at the end, she hadn't been able to *be* with him in any meaningful way. Hadn't been able to talk to him or explain the dark place she'd gone to. Her heart had broken, her body and mind had shut down to everything but grief and a resentment she'd known, even then, she had no right to…and yet couldn't fight. The shame, sorrow and anger had eaten her alive until all she could do was close herself off from everyone and everything. All she could do was leave. Try not to look back, because she couldn't stand to see whether it was relief or betrayal shining in Ryan's eyes as he watched her go.

"So what are you resolving?"

That was the question. Maybe nothing. Maybe she was simply filling in the hole where saying goodbye should have happened.

Sally huffed at her silence. "Claire, call your lawyer and have him work out the settlement for you. What you're doing is a mistake."

"How can you even say that? You've never even met Ryan, let alone seen us together. We're going into this with our eyes open. Believe me."

"What I believe is that you're even worse off than I thought. I don't have to meet Ryan to know what a threat he is to you. For God's sake, *I know you.* I've seen the way you live your life and I've seen your face each time his picture splashes across some tabloid cover."

Claire bristled, pushing off the couch. "You don't know what you're talking about. Yes, I care about Ryan, and I will for the rest of my life. But that doesn't mean I'm suffering some delusion about a future together. This is closure."

"This is an affair. *You're lovers.*"

"Only until we settle."

"And then what? You watch him walk away while your heart is breaking all over again?"

"No. We both walk away."

"And your heart?" Sally's heavy sigh filled the line. "You don't have affairs, Claire. You aren't casual. How can you believe you'll be able to spend all this time with the man you loved enough to marry, and not fall again?"

"Because I know better!" she snapped back, unable to listen to another question, challenge or charge. Unwilling to acknowledge them because, regardless of how well founded they might be, Claire wasn't going to stop. She couldn't.

A pause, and then, "Well, I guess you know what you're doing."

"I do."

The call ended a few strained minutes later. Claire set down the phone and returned to the window, studying the new accumulation that covered the neighborhood landscape in a pristine blanket of white. It looked soft and fresh and so inviting. And yet only a fool would risk jumping in. A mere inch beneath the surface lay the remains of the winter's past. Brittle, jagged and dirty. Until all that had come before was cleared away, the new snow wouldn't be anything but a dangerous temptation, one better to avoid.

Closing her eyes, Claire let her head fall back and the muscles of her neck lengthen and stretch. She wanted to forget about the snow altogether, hop on a plane back to California and lose herself in the sun. The vastness of the ocean. The steeped hills. And most of all, in Ryan's arms.

They'd spent two nights together. Two nights and one incredible day. Their progress with the assets had been minimal at best. Barely more than a return of the files scattered across the dining room floor to their state prior to that first combustible kiss.

But neither of them was concerned. They'd manage a better balance the next time, once they burned a bit of that initial intensity off between the sheets.

Another trip to California. Another chauffeured ride to the beach house, though this one alone.

Claire's schedule had been solid for the next three months—the way she'd become accustomed to booking it. But knowing the assets had to be dealt with sooner or later, she'd done some juggling to make it work. And Ryan had done the same, providing this Sunday-to-Tuesday window to see what progress could be made. The way she figured it, they'd focus on the asset division during the day and leave the evenings for... recreation.

The time and distance had helped her regain her perspective, solidifying the boundaries of what they were doing together. She'd thought about Ryan, of course. Probably more than she should have, but it had been impossible not to. Her restored libido seemed to be making up for lost time, running full steam through both waking and sleeping hours. So, yes, Ryan had been on her mind plenty. But in a physiological way, rather than one that was emotionally dependent.

She wouldn't forget this was an *affair*, not some *affair of the heart*. Neither of them would. A point underscored by the limited exchange of a few impersonal emails coordinating plans over the two weeks since they'd parted ways. And Ryan hadn't even met her at the airport, proving all those warning glares Sally sent her off with unnecessary.

The car cut over to the exit ramp and Claire's pulse skipped a beat. Glancing at the uncluttered seat around her, she realized she hadn't even taken her computer out of its tote. Her phone remained tucked into its pocket in her purse, and she'd spent the last twenty-five minutes thinking only of Ryan like some kind of crazed schoolgirl obsessing over her crush. That wasn't the kind of hold she wanted him to have over her, but this was the first trip since they'd decided to pursue the affair, so of course she'd been distracted, anticipating what it would be like after two weeks apart. For all she knew, that crazy chemistry they couldn't resist the last time they were together wouldn't be the same. If that turned out to be the case, she'd handle it. God, she just hoped she didn't have to.

The electronic gate opened ahead of her and the car pulled through. Ryan stood off to the left of the carport, feet braced apart, legs clad in dark trousers, dress shirt open at the neck and rolled to midforearm, hands knuckled at his hips. Dark eyes hot as they locked on her through the window.

Chemistry. The kind that syphoned the oxygen from the air and charged the molecules within it until they started to burn.

Claire pulled her purse over her shoulder and reached for her computer bag, taking the extra seconds to ground the nerves that had suddenly gone haywire. Only, then, the car door swung open and Ryan was leaning into her space, pressing her back into the cushions of the seat as his lips closed over hers with a ravenous claim.

Her eyes closed beneath the assault, blocking out all but Ryan and the clean spicy scent of him. The heat of his hand curling around her neck. And the taste of his tongue moving against hers.

Sensual, slow strokes that had her arching into his chest, opening wider to his possession and slipping her fingers into the short silk of his hair. Her nipples rasped tight against her bra, and she pressed into his chest, in search of the relief only intimate contact could offer. His low groan rolled over her tongue, filling her mouth with a need that matched her own.

Ryan broke from the kiss, gently pulling free even as she tugged to pull him back.

Disappointment crashed through her like a wrecking ball at his rough "No."

And then that smile broke across his lips and his head dropped forward with a weary shake. "*This* is why I didn't pick you up at the airport."

Claire blinked. Once in confusion, and then in quick repetition as, shocked, she recalled their particular circumstances.

Her breath sucked in and Ryan offered what might be an amused nod. Though at second glance, the lines of strain etched around his face suggested perhaps *pained* would more accurately describe it.

In the span of those few seconds, they'd ended up half sprawled across the backseat with Claire's skirt hiked to the very limits of propriety and the spike of her heel braced against the back of Ryan's calf. Meanwhile, the driver in the front shifted awkwardly in his seat, eyes averted, but judging by the plum stain across his neck, cheeks and ears…acutely aware of the goings-on behind him.

Ryan growled low in his throat. He ought to be jumping off her, backing out of the car and ushering her into the house. But the evidence of why he wasn't prodded steadily at her thigh.

Claire glanced desperately around them and, finding her purse, shot out a hand to grab it. Holding it in the tight space between them, she offered it up with a single raised brow. Ryan rolled his eyes with a muttered "Please." Then fixed on something just behind her, satisfaction lighting his features. Grabbing her computer bag, he held it up in counter and backed out of the car even as Claire collapsed back in a gale of laughter.

But then that warm palm was smoothing up her thigh, fixing her skirt, before taking her hand to draw her up. "Out of the car now. As it is, the tip this little indiscretion is going to cost me will be paying for orthodontics for Mickey's daughter. Another minute of your rolling around back here and I'll be paying off his house."

Claire allowed herself to be pulled free of the car and headed straight into the house as Ryan took care of her bags and the orthodontic bill. Heart soaring with all concerns about waning chemistry incinerated beneath that kiss, she skipped up the stairs, dropping her blouse at the third step, and her skirt at the seventh. Seconds later, the front door closed and Ryan's heavy footfall sounded over the steps. "If you want the bed, baby, you better get there before I get to you."

Claire gauged the last flight, Ryan's ability to navigate encumbered as he was, and her skill in three-inch sling backs—and set off with a squeal.

CHAPTER THIRTEEN

IN the war against temptation, Ryan was fighting a losing
battle. They'd been back at it, buried in property assessments,
earnings reports and development proposals, for an hour already and, by rights, Ryan ought to have cleared triple what he
had. Instead, he'd found his gaze wandering across the spread
of divorce headquarters time and again. And even when he'd
ruthlessly dragged it back, his mind wouldn't cooperate.

Claire had dressed in another one of those filmy sleeveless
tops. A coral-colored fluttery silk concoction that managed
to be sweet and suggestive all at once. A matching scarf hung
loose and low around her neck. It was ridiculous, a scarf with
a sleeveless blouse of all the damn things in the world. And
why that should get under his skin he had no idea except
maybe for the fact he could only think of one reason a scarf
like that might come in handy and it didn't have anything to
do with fashionable accenting.

Claire stretched her arms overhead, linking her fingers
in a way that only fed the depraved nature of his thoughts.
Then, slipping out of her seat, she carried her empty water
glass over to the wet bar. White tie waist pants sat low on her
hips and his palms itched to mold over the rounded bottom
they flattered. She'd been there for two days already. This
frenzied need should have worn off. Hell, he'd expected it to
wear off after the first night of having her back in his bed—or

at least cool down to the point where he could get through a morning's worth of work without losing his concentration to what she had on and how quickly he could get it off. Get her mind and legs wrapped around him, and that smart mouth of hers coming at him from every direction.

"We have to work on this stuff sometime," Claire said, her elbows resting on the bar behind her, refilled glass in hand. The stance was relaxed, but the look in her eyes was alert. Aware. She knew exactly where his thoughts had traveled. A skill not many people could claim.

"We're working now."

"Are we? You look…distracted."

A subtle tension slipped through his shoulders, knotting tight at his neck. He didn't get distracted by his dates. He didn't blow off business to spend time with them. He didn't mercilessly plot all the ways he could get them naked and wrapped around him. He just didn't care like this and it didn't make any sense.

Except it did.

Because he'd been here before.

In the beginning, this was what it had been like with Claire. He'd wanted to eat, drink, sleep and screw her with his every breath. *In the beginning.*

And then later—hell. Later, he couldn't wait to get away.

It was that thought that had him ignoring the flare of interest in Claire's blue eyes and working to focus on the task at hand. "The Austin properties are up next."

Claire's nose wrinkled, but she didn't try to sway him. Except, perhaps, with an extra turn to her hips as she crossed back to the table. Or maybe he was just watching more closely.

Sweeping a pencil from the open file in front of him, he walked it through the fingers of one hand to keep from reaching for her as she brushed past and humphed back into her chair with a little pout that had him wanting to shove the files off the table and lay Claire out atop it. Work his mouth over every inch of her, starting at her toes, until that pretty little pout gave up his name on a sultry moan.

Forget moan. He'd make her *scream*.

Only they'd lost hours making sense of the files he'd spilled across the floor on her first visit and he wasn't about to do it again.

Except the way she kept playing with the ends of that scarf—twirling it around her fingers, letting is slip around her wrists—

The pencil snapped.

"Ryan?"

His gaze shot from Claire to the splintered shards in his hand and then back.

He needed to stop thinking about sex. He was worse than a teenager. It was like some switch had been flipped and his brain was running a 24/7 sexstravaganza. He'd become a slave to his libido, and he wasn't even the one coming off a dry spell. It was embarrassing.

But worse than that, it wasn't just the sex. It was everything. The talking. The laughing. The stories about her gallery and the struggles that got her to where she was with it. He couldn't get enough of this woman Claire was now. The heady combination of who she'd been and who she'd become was intoxicating…addictive.

And he didn't want to get hooked.

Which meant he couldn't give in to every impulse pumping through his veins. He needed to regain control and remember that, no matter how good this felt, it wasn't going to last. It hadn't before, when he would have bet his life it would, and, though they were different people, he knew better than to believe it would now.

His jaw set and the shards of a broken number two

threatened to embed in his palms. He pushed to his feet, tossing the pencil to the trash without a glance.

"The Austin properties?" Claire prompted again, her fingertips drifting lazily around the hollow at the base of her throat. "In case you…you know…forgot or something."

And now she was taunting him. "Thanks for that. But, no. I didn't forget."

Control. That was the crux of it. Physically speaking, that was a slippery slope he was willing to navigate. If he lost his traction and went down, he wouldn't be alone and there were a hell of a lot worse things than Claire landing on top of him. But emotionally, now, that was a susceptibility worth guarding against.

Flipping the topmost file open, Ryan rolled his shoulders and blew out a tight breath. "The Austin properties."

A pencil tapped against the table in a rapid staccato, calling his attention back to Claire, who'd pinned him with a level stare. "Already there. Try to keep up, would you?" The corners of her mouth twitched, and then gave in to a full grin. The kind that made him want to know how far he could push it. What it would take to earn the laugh that rang like music through his memories.

And then he was leaning forward, elbows on the table. "So you want to play, huh?"

Her brow arched, challenge shining in her eyes. He didn't have a chance. He'd been staring right at her, plotting his best defense—and already she'd gotten to him.

The following week, Ryan strode out to the terrace, offering his phone as he set their bag of takeout on the table. "Check the open news clip."

Claire stood from where she'd been resting on a lounge chair and walked over, snickering as she read. "Where do you get this stuff?"

"Nutty news feed. Keeps things light."

Ryan rifled through the bag for the jalapeño chips and watched in anticipation as Claire scrolled through the article, the grin on her face stretching wider as the seconds passed.

Finally she shook her head and handed back the phone, grinning. "That's funny. So this is how you convince everyone you're so busy all the time? Keeping your nose buried in these snazzy little phone applications with weird news feeds?"

Ryan popped a chip into his mouth, chewing around his words. "And games. The work is all a ruse. I'm the Bejeweled national champion this week."

"Being the genuine hard worker I am, slacker—" she paused for effect, batting her lashes at him "—I don't even know what Bejeweled is."

"Now, *that's* criminal. I'll load it on your phone for you."

"No, thanks. *You're* distracting me enough as it is."

Ryan flashed his teeth at her, all cocky, bad-boy charm and proud of it. "Am I?"

"You don't have to be so delighted!" She laughed, casting around for a set down and grasping at the first thing she found. "After all, you're just a temporary distraction."

Jaw shifting out of line, he nodded amused understanding. "Whereas what you've got going on with the phone…is a long-term thing."

"Exactly. It works," she said, waving a chip at him. "Don't mess with it."

Ryan leaned into the chair watching her from across the table with a subtle smile playing over his lips.

These were the dangerous moments, the ones where they were as comfortable with gull's cries and rushing waves filling the air between them as they were with the conversation that came as easily as if they'd never let it fall away. The ones that were so quiet and unassuming, they caught her unawares. Slipping stealthily beneath her skin, expanding with a physical pressure until she wondered if it was pleasure or pain that had her at the point of bursting.

Wondering how she was going to give this up again.

The quiet strains of a moody love song cut through her thoughts, originating from the phone she loosely held in her lap.

Ryan's brow slammed down, his lazy posture going alert. "Here, pass that over."

Claire automatically began to hand the phone across the table, but then she caught the contact picture displaying the caller and her fingers clamped down. She knew those soft grey eyes and that nearly too wide smile, just like the rest of the country and probably the world did as well. Dahlia Dawson.

Ryan's ex. The actress he'd been seeing on and off for the past two years. The one with whom Ryan had promised things were over. Not just off-again. But here she was calling and suddenly Claire's heart was in her throat, her stomach twisting into anxious knots.

Only, *she had no right.*

Forcing herself to relax her hold, she held out the small device. "It's for you, I think," she offered stupidly.

Who else? It was his phone. His ex.

Ryan took the device without a word, sending the call straight to voice mail.

"You aren't going to answer it?" She wanted to cry at the thin sound of her voice and the tremble tingeing her words.

"No. I wouldn't do that to you. Or her," he said, meeting her with a level stare. "I'll call back later."

Of course not. Ryan wasn't the kind of man to treat some- one cruelly or be casual with their feelings. It had always been that way with him and it had always been something she'd respected. Only now, she couldn't help wondering what that courtesy meant for them and when exactly *later* would be?

Would he wait until she was in the shower? Excuse himself from the room after a meal. Would she be left watching the door as her husband walked through it to call his girlfriend?

The hot lick of shame scorched her cheeks, and she nearly choked as that last thought registered.

Ryan was not her husband. Not in any of the ways that mattered and certainly not because of what was happening between them now.

His stare hardened. "It's over with Dahlia. I told you. So whatever you're thinking, stop."

She didn't know what she was thinking except that everything seemed more fragile and temporary than it had a few moments ago. As if the winds had shifted, taking that balmy comfortable breeze with it, and blowing in an uncertainty Claire had no right to feel.

She'd known about the other women, both real and fabricated, for years. They hadn't bothered her beyond the most mild irritation. Mostly anyway. But now, her gaze moved over the planes of Ryan's face, the bulk of his shoulders and power of his arms. She studied the length and width of his fingers, the bronze of his skin and the crisp dark hairs of his forearms. She thought about the way he'd run his hands over her bare hip after they'd made love the night before. The way his gruff laugh sounded at her ear when she'd teased him.

She'd begun looking at Ryan and thinking, *"Mine."*

He had been, once upon a time. But not anymore. In the years since they'd been apart, he'd belonged to other women.

And she was jealous.

Not so much that they'd had his body, though at this moment she was decidedly less than thrilled about that, but that they'd had his heart. *His affection.* A part of him apparently she'd still thought of as hers.

"Claire?"

She peered up at him, somewhat stunned by her revelation. "You know, as crazy as this may sound, I think a part of me was more comfortable believing all those tabloid reports about you and your exploits."

Ryan's frown deepened and he leaned forward in his chair. "Why's that?"

"If you'd become some womanizing jerk who couldn't keep his pants zipped, it would be easier for me to convince myself there hadn't been anyone…special. That what we had was unique."

Ryan stared at her, the dark brown of his eyes fixed and unreadable. Maybe telling him had been as selfish as the thoughts themselves. Maybe more.

She wasn't supposed to want to keep him as her own. That wasn't the point of what they were doing together.

Pushing back from the table, Ryan picked up his plate and turned to the house. Well, really, what could she expect him to say in response to a statement like that? It didn't merit a defense. And yet watching him walk off without a word cut her to the core.

Ryan stopped at the door, his steps halting in a way that suggested hesitation over conviction. His head dropped a degree, angling to where she could see his features but not meet his eyes. "I didn't marry any of them."

Claire was gone and Ryan was back in the L.A. office working late to make up for the time he'd been taking off around her visits. It was already after nine, but he'd easily be putting in a few more hours before calling it a night. This had just been a quick break to let the delivery guy in, plow through a turkey-and-avocado on whole grain and try a callback to Dahlia.

She hadn't answered, which wasn't any surprise. She'd been impossible to connect with, even when they'd been together.

And while it hadn't particularly bothered him then, it did now. Because it wasn't like her to call. It didn't make sense.

She wouldn't pursue a reconciliation. Not the way they'd left things.

And her PR manager had always been the one to contact him when there was a delicate media response to handle. So why, when they hadn't been in touch in months and they'd both managed to stay relatively out of the news, had she decided to call now?

CHAPTER FOURTEEN

ANOTHER week, another visit.

Progress on the asset division was coming steady but slow. Without a definitive deadline looming, they'd fallen into the habit of taking mornings off to enjoy a bit of local activity—jogging on the beach, exploring the tide pools, walking the caves at the cove, or taking their coffee over to surfing hot spot Windansea...something—anything—to act as a buffer between leaving bed and hitting divorce headquarters.

Today, it was the La Jolla Open Aire Market, around which parking was always tight, so Ryan had let Claire out at the front gate while he looked for a spot. Catching sight of a woman loading her stroller into the back of her SUV half a block down Girard, Ryan waited for her to drive off and then pulled in. Not bad.

Hopping out, he jogged back to the chain-link-fence opening that led into the elementary school playground that housed the market each Sunday. Within seconds, he had Claire in sight. She would have stood out with her raven-dark ponytail, navy ball cap and authentically distressed, orange T-shirt regardless, but somehow in the last month, his internal compass had started pointing due Claire again.

Strange, the things that came back. More so, the things he'd been surprised to realize hadn't gone away.

Closing the distance between them, he skimmed his palm

over that dangerous stretch of exposed skin above the low ride of her jeans and high hem of her shirt. "Knew I'd find you here."

Claire cast him a quick glance, her eyes bright, before returning her attention to the stand where bucket upon flower-filled bucket created a spectrum of vibrant hues, blossoms and buds that looked nearly as petal soft as the skin his fingers brushed.

"The sunflowers, I think," she said, pointing to her selection with a satisfied smile that left Ryan wondering how it was that every male within one hundred feet hadn't stopped to gawk. Though on second glance, more than a few actually had. He couldn't blame them.

When Claire went for her money, he rolled his eyes, leaning in close to her ear as he stilled her hand. "Let's call this a date, okay? Why don't you let me buy you some flowers and a meal?"

"A date?"

He could hear the smile in her voice and knew at last he'd hit the jackpot. "Yeah. Been a while since we had one."

Ryan exchanged a few bills for the sunburst bouquet wrapped in old news, and handed it over to Claire, who smiled up at him from beneath her lashes with what unbelievably looked like a shy blush pinkening her cheeks.

His heart turned over with a heavy thud at the sight of it.

"Thank you, Ryan."

Damn, he could barely manage the noncommittal grunt, let alone try for words when she looked at him like that. When that pretty pink slid through his veins, warming them with something that wasn't quite lust.

Swallowing hard, he ushered her farther into the maze of merchants, hoping that amid the artisans, farm stands and bakery stalls, she wouldn't notice that the man beside her had gone stupid over one sweet blush.

It was just the kind of reaction he'd been doing his damnedest to avoid. But there it was. And his only consolation was that Claire would be gone tomorrow. Back to her life in New York and apart from him. For at least another two weeks.

So what if she got to him more than he'd wanted to let her. The time they spent together was a fraction of what they spent apart and regardless of whatever feelings those little smiles stirred up in him, they both knew this relationship wasn't destined to go the distance. In all honesty, it probably only felt as good as it did because of the limits they'd imposed on it.

The paradise factor. When they were together, they were both outside their real lives. Outside their normal environment. La Jolla had always been his escape, and that's what it was with Claire. A place where real life hadn't invaded.

Nothing messy.

Nothing but fun.

Even if that wasn't it, they still couldn't get in too deep for the simple fact there wasn't time. Slow as the progress might be, they were making it. One of these weeks, probably within the next month, the settlement would be complete and then the divorce would follow. And this time with Claire would be over.

No, he wasn't looking forward to that day.

He glanced down at her walking beside him, captivating even at her most casual, and wondered how he'd ever thought he had a chance at defending against this.

Maybe if he'd known the effect she would have on him… no, he still would have gone to Rome to get her. Only then he wouldn't have bothered to keep his distance; he'd have used every trick in the book to get her beneath him before they even left her suite. And then again on the jet. Definitely the jet.

One playful bump of a hip against his had his thoughts

plummeting from mile high to the delighted blue eyes gazing up at him.

"This is an incredible market. So many temptations all in one place."

"Yeah, which ones are you finding the hardest to resist?"

She pointed out several vendors, her weaknesses running the gamut from decadent pastries, to handmade soaps, hanging tapestries and everything in between. Ryan glanced around, enjoying the market with new eyes as Claire cut a slow path through the crowd until they'd passed the food court and come to an open lawn area. More stands lined the perimeter, and at the center people gathered to eat picnic style in the grass while listening to a female soloist who played the guitar and sang in a voice so melodic it begged listeners to close their eyes and lie down.

"Hungry?" he asked, getting that way himself. "You could sit and I'll bring something back."

Claire's hand slipped over her stomach, and for an instant Ryan's world screeched to a halt. Too many memories associated with that gesture for his peace of mind. But she'd merely rubbed a palm over the flat plane and shrugged. "Actually, I'm starving. What's good here?"

A few minutes later Ryan returned balancing three flimsy trays of the best Mexican this side of the border, with a couple of waters pinned under his arm. He scanned the crowd, looking for the gorgeous brunette tucked beneath the Cubs cap she'd snagged from his closet that morning. A hoot of laughter caught his attention from the far end of the market. Before he turned, he knew.

Hula hoops.

A wide grassy expanse behind the last row of booths was dotted with females of every age, race, shape and ability. Each swiveling her hips with a smile that sparkled as brightly as the elaborately decorated hoop making its revolutions around her hips. And there in the center was Claire.

That too-small-to-begin-with T-shirt riding around her ribs. Jeans dangerously low. Arms up, her sunflowers carefully set off to the side. Her hips—God help him—moving in slow undulations that emphasized the slim strength in her belly and instantly set his body to respond. He swallowed. Hard. And walked to the edge of the hula grounds.

Claire glanced up, eyes gleaming with mirth when she caught his expression. "You like it. I know you do."

He offered a stiff nod. "Just come and get the money out of my pocket. We're buying it."

Claire arched a brow and, stopping inches too close, slipped her hand into his front pocket, snickering when he glared a warning after the first graze of her fingers against him.

"You're about two seconds from lunch going into the trash and you and your hula hoop going over my shoulder."

"Oooh," she teased, stroking her fingers to run the length of him again. "Big man...with all those threats."

The tacos nearly hit the ground with the clench of his fist, but Claire, giggling wickedly, was quick on the extraction and managed to help him rebalance the trays before they were lost.

"You're a very, very bad girl."

Another impish wink. She knew it. Hell, she was reveling in it. "So spank me."

Ryan's jaw clenched tight, and the popping sound of his molars threatening to grind down to dust forced him to look away. God help him, the minute he got her alone he would.

Seated within the circle of her spectacular new hula hoop, the remnants of their lunch stacked beside her, Claire squinted into the pale blue sky above. "So why La Jolla?"

Ryan cocked his head and turned a lopsided smile her way. "You've seen it. I'm surprised you need to ask."

A gentle breeze tickled her neck and ears. "No, I see how beautiful it is. But it's not exactly part of Silicon Valley or a hotbed of investment opportunity, at least of the variety you seem drawn to. So how'd you find it?"

"A friend introduced me to the place a few years back. It's close enough to L.A. that the drive is more than manageable, but far enough to get away from the chaos."

Fingering a thick blade of grass, Claire asked, "Hollywood chaos?"

The barest pause and then, "Yes."

Claire nodded, glancing away.

His actress girlfriend had brought him down here to get away from the hubbub. And he'd enjoyed it enough to build a place of his own.

What a different world he lived in. At times she wondered how she recognized him at all, except, even as different as his life had become...he was so much the same man. The man she'd fallen for too hard. Depended on too much. Treated too unfairly. The man she'd never completely gotten over—no matter what lies she'd been telling herself all this time.

"Claire—"

"I can definitely understand the draw," she cut him off with an encompassing wave of her hand. She shouldn't have asked about Hollywood. Didn't want to know any more than she already did about Dahlia. Whether he'd been talking to her again. If they'd remained friends.

Teasingly, she drove the point home with a flirty wink. "If my ex didn't have a place down here, I might consider it for myself."

"Oh, yeah? Think you could afford it?"

She leaned conspiratorially toward him. "I'm coming into a bit of cash."

Ryan chuckled, leaning back on his arms. "Not until we settle."

"You in a rush?"

"No. It has to get done, but I'm not in any rush."

Searching Ryan's eyes, she found easy understanding in them. The warm comfort of a connection not completely dead. Softly, she answered, "Then neither am I."

Together they stretched back into the bed of grass and, blanketed by the sun's warm rays, listened to the midday lullaby of music and laughter mingling around them.

It might have been a half hour, or maybe only ten minutes, but briefly time and space and the weight of the world disappeared and there'd been only the contentment of drifting in the plane between sleep and wake.

Refreshed, Claire sat up, tucking her legs to one side. Ryan lay beside her, his breath coming slow and regular. Sleeping. She could see it in the relaxed lines of his chiseled face. Sense it in the quiet between them.

Her hand moved to the center of his chest, and she closed her eyes. Felt the steady *thump, thump* of his heart beat beneath her fingertips, wrap around her nerve endings and wind in a rhythmic pulse through her arm until his vitality mingled at the very heart of her own.

Something swelled deep inside her. Strained against the confines she'd thought to impose—thought would keep her safe. And pushed words she couldn't say—didn't want to acknowledge—toward her lips.

I love you.

She tamped them back, relegating them to the dark corners of her mind. The places where threadbare hopes and tattered dreams cluttered the background of her consciousness with all that might have been. Swing sets, family dinners and lives that grew together rather than apart.

Things she couldn't have and knew better than to want.

The heat of Ryan's hand covered her own and she jerked back to sever the connection. But he held her steady, pressed her palm into the place where she'd let it rest.

"Stay. Lie down with me again. This is too perfect to give up just yet."

Claire nodded. It *was* too perfect to give up just yet. Even if it was just the fantasy that Ryan meant *them*, rather than a few last minutes beneath the warm sun.

CHAPTER FIFTEEN

CLAIRE's disposition had been foul to begin with. They'd had to cancel her flight out west the previous weekend due to some crisis with a deal Ryan had been working and they'd yet to sync their schedules for another time.

And then this disaster at the gallery.

Sally had called before eight in a panic with the news that somehow the next two weeks of Claire's calendar had been lost to the void of cyberspace. She'd spent the day playing catch-up, making apologies and bumbling appointments she would normally have been fully prepared for. Eleven hours later, she'd been ready to drop. Both mentally and physically exhausted. Frustrated to be so out of control.

And then Aaron showed up. His usual affable self, brightening her day with quirky anecdotes and tickets for a show they'd agreed to see months ago. Another misplaced appointment— but this one she could easily accommodate. Aaron Kinner was a client she'd enjoyed a limited social relationship with over the years thanks to their shared taste in theater, art and music. They connected every few months when he was in town, taking in a show or exhibit, always something casual. Always fun.

As burnt as she'd been, she couldn't turn him down.

They'd discussed the production over a late dinner and laughed their way through coffee and dessert. The evening turned out to be enjoyable and nearly distracting enough to keep Claire's mind off Ryan, the fact that she wasn't with him, and just how badly she wished she were.

Nearly.

"You seem different tonight," Aaron offered with a sidelong glance as they waited for the light to cross.

The New York spring day had been warm, but with the sun long ago set, the temperature had once again dropped. And even bundled in wool, Claire shivered, rubbing her hands over her arms. "Different?"

"Yeah, but don't get that wrinkled-little-brow thing going." The light changed and Aaron's hand moved lightly to the small of her back as they crossed the intersection. "Different good."

She didn't quite know what to make of that. She certainly felt different. Things had been changing within her since that first night with Ryan. But she hadn't expected anyone to see it beyond herself.

"Like your smile's running a little deeper." He shrugged, stuffing his hands into his trench-coat pockets. "I like it."

They slowed at the walk to Claire's apartment and she turned toward Aaron, extending her hand for the friendly shake they'd always exchanged. Only this time when Aaron took it, he didn't let go, but rather turned her hand in his as though examining it, while waffling his head in a show of indecision.

Claire began to laugh, wondering what he was up to. But when his eyes met hers, her stomach dropped with the realization he wasn't playing a game.

"I like it a lot, Claire."

Before she could formulate a protest, he'd ducked down, catching her mouth with his kiss as he locked one arm across the small of her back.

Three things struck her in short order. The first, she should have seen this coming. If her attention hadn't been split between where she was and where she'd wanted to be—in Ryan's arms—she might have noticed a shift in Aaron's behavior. The second, an almost clinical observation that, while Aaron was undoubtedly an attractive man, the cool press of his lips left her utterly unaffected. The only response stirred, the increasing need to end contact. And third, they weren't alone.

A voice broke through the night around them.

"Claire." One word, barely restrained, threatening to her on every level.

She froze in her spot, stalling even her efforts to break away. But her name must have been enough to catch Aaron's attention because as quickly as he'd caught her, he set her back with a chuckled whisper about being busted.

The man had no idea.

"Ryan." Crazy elation whipped through her at the knowledge *he was there*, then landed with a crack of horror. He'd just watched another man kiss her, pull her flush against his body as though he owned her. And she hadn't even managed a single *no* before he'd interrupted them.

Her lips felt numb, her throat dry as she turned.

Ryan stood a few paces off, his flat eyes and deceptively casual stance betrayed only by the ticking muscle in his jaw.

She wanted to rush to his side and throw her arms around his neck. Tell him that kiss had been nothing but the misunderstanding of a friend, but she couldn't move. Aaron needed to understand there would be nothing between them, but here in front of Ryan wasn't the time to make that clarification.

Only with both men standing before her, one staring at her expectantly, the other… Well, she didn't quite know what to make of the look on Ryan's face. Or she didn't until Aaron's arm looped over her shoulders and the eyes that had been flat seconds ago went lethal.

Quickly, she stepped aside. "Aaron, thank you for tonight. Again, I'm so sorry about the scheduling problem and forgetting our tickets. I'll call you in the next week."

Aaron grinned down at her, as if the idea of his leaving was ludicrous. Then turning his attention back to Ryan, furrowed his brow before giving his forehead a smack. "Wait, Ryan Brady, right?"

Oblivious to the precariousness of his situation, he stepped past her, arm outstretched in greeting. "Aaron Kinner. We met at the *Lansing* premiere last fall. Didn't recognize you at first."

Ryan shook his hand, and then—thankfully—released it without incident. Or a word.

Pausing, Aaron shot a quizzical glance between her and Ryan. *"Brady?"*

Claire felt the air go thin around her as the foundation of her world begin to crumble.

"You two aren't related, are you?"

Ryan's lips twisted into a wry smile as he stepped forward and blatantly tugged Claire into his hold, resting a possessive arm around her shoulders. "Through marriage."

The answer seemed to both satisfy and delight Aaron, while shocking Claire into stunned silence.

"Phew. Explains the whole 'protective big brother' vibe. You know, 'break her heart and I'll break your face' thing."

The flash of straight white teeth against the shadows of night had Claire's blood running cold as that twisted smile broke into a full grin. Not so Aaron, who apparently didn't have a single ounce of survival instinct and was punching the air with a few awkward jabs.

"Something like that," Ryan answered, his tone devoid of humor. "Only, I'm not her brother."

Aaron stalled midpunch, his expression hesitant as he looked between them. Straightened and went still. He knew.

Claire felt the color rise to her cheeks and, unable to handle the scrutiny, let her gaze drift around the pointed toes of her shoes. "Thank you again, Aaron. For being so understanding about tonight."

He would never speak to her again after this. Though, in light of that kiss, perhaps it was for the best.

"Yeah, sure thing, Claire. I'll call."

A moment later Aaron was on his way and Ryan and Claire were left in the cold and quiet of her apartment stoop, staring at the empty walk ahead of them.

It was Ryan who moved first, catching her by the lapel of her coat and towing her slowly toward her door.

Her steps dragged and her belly churned in anxious knots at the idea of the confrontation to come.

"Keys, Claire. Unless you've changed your stance on public declarations and displays of affection. Your boyfriend certainly seemed to think so."

Oh, God, there it was. The first jab, not that she could blame him. "We're just friends."

"Exactly how many *friends* like that do you have?" The arch of Ryan's brow reminding her of the kiss itself.

"None. Or, at least I didn't think so. He's never even hinted at an attraction before, but tonight he said I seemed…different. I didn't realize he'd interpreted *different* as an invitation." She shook her head, those big blue eyes imploring him to believe. *"Misinterpreted."*

"I get it." Ryan slipped his hands into the pockets of Claire's overcoat, drawing her against him as he fished for the keys she'd been too distracted to search for.

Nothing. Nothing but a layer closer to the body he wanted in to. "I do."

The way her eyes had flown open and her face pinched up at the kiss had said everything her mouth hadn't been able to. If that Aaron had opened his eyes for two-tenths of a second he would have seen it too. But the guy had been too caught up in what he wanted to happen.

It hadn't been pretty.

Which explained why Ryan wasn't icing a broken knuckle and scheduling someone to patch a nearby wall. There'd been no mistaking Claire's response—not interested.

Not this time anyway. Not this guy.

But what struck him—and with the unpleasant force of a battering ram to the gut—was that he was witnessing a preview of things to come. Of the way it *could* happen. Another man stepping in to claim what had for so long been his and his alone.

And, damn it, he didn't like it.

Something hot and demanding stirred inside him. A waking urgency that tensed his muscles and tightened his spine.

Claire was beautiful. Vivacious. And…available in a way she hadn't been when he'd first found her in Rome.

What Aaron had said about her being different. It was true.

Something had changed in her. Around her. As if the invisible shield she'd erected, unseen but easily sensed, had been knocked down, making her accessible. Approachable.

She'd been alone all this time because she hadn't been able to take that last step into intimacy. Because she hadn't been able to *feel*. Well, she could feel now. He'd have her *feeling* six times before the night was through…just as soon as he got his hands on those keys and got them inside.

Maybe her purse. He had the clutch out from under her arm and open in no time.

Rattling the fob between them, he let out a whoop. "Jackpot!"

Claire blinked up at him. "You're not upset?"

Ryan stilled in his efforts to maneuver them inside. A group of raucous pedestrians passed by, laughing as they huddled together. Looking back into Claire's face, he caught her chin in the loose frame of his fingers.

"Not upset." Not now. He knew she hadn't encouraged the kiss and Aaron hadn't been any kind of threat. Not to either of them. "But, I won't lie, seeing another guy touch you is doing something to me I don't like. Which is why I'm trying to get us inside."

Her chin pulled back, and her voice went low. "So you can yell?"

Hell.

"No." His jaw clamped down and his breath whistled through his teeth. "So when I take you against the wall, before you even have a chance to get your jacket off, because I have to prove to myself that, for now, you're still mine—your whole neighborhood won't be watching."

Her breath caught on a quiver, her pupils dilated, turning the deep blue of her eyes into a bottomless well of temptation. "I'm still yours."

Not enough. The words weren't enough. Not when her slight hands smoothed over his chest, across his shoulders and around his neck to tangle into his hair. Not when her hips rocked against him in blatant invitation of everything he was asking for.

His hands clenched with the need to take. To claim. To mark.

To make sure no other man mistook her for anything but belonging to *him*.

Another rock of her hips and sharp tug at his hair. Demanding.

Yes. This was his girl. Taunting him with everything he wanted, pushing the limits of his control, and all but begging him to give it to her. The keys dug into his palm.

Towing Claire against him with one arm, he jammed the key into the lock and pushed inside.

* * *

Slumped against the door, legs extended over the hardwood entry, Ryan ran a hand through his sweat-matted hair.

Damn, this was insane. Not just that he'd spent more time sprawled over flooring in the past month and a half than he had in years, but that he'd come to New York at all. He'd been going nuts since his deal began to implode the week before and he'd had to cancel out on seeing Claire.

While it wasn't the first time business had shot a hole through his personal plans, it was the first time he'd been ready to take someone apart over it. But he'd put business first. Gotten a handle on the deal and gotten on with his daily existence…almost.

The problem was, every day he was getting more unreasonable. More agitated. He wanted to see Claire, but their schedules didn't mesh. And finally, after a night devoid of sleep, he'd given up and decided to make the trip to New York.

He—and everyone with a shred of hope for their continued relationship with him—pushed meetings and manipulated schedules and overall made sure everything that had to get done got done fast. He'd been a tyrant. But it had worked and he'd gotten what he wanted.

Claire in his arms.

A kitten-soft mewl sounded beneath his chin and Claire planted one hand against his chest, her cashmere scarf hanging drunkenly from her wrist as she pushed back from where she'd collapsed against him. A single button on her coat remained secure, though somehow she'd managed to work an arm free. Her skirt rode around her hips, the silk lapels of her blouse hanging open to reveal the cups of her bra bunched below her breasts.

He'd done it. Marked her. Left a half-dollar-size hickey at the tender slope of her breast.

He ought to be disgusted, but pure possessive male satisfaction won the day.

The night. Whenever it was.

Checking his watch, he let out a low chuckle.

Eyeing him beneath heavy lids, Claire demanded, "What's so funny?"

Ryan ran his palms up the bare skin of her thighs and cupped her bottom, holding her close where their bodies were still connected. "An hour, and we still haven't made it farther than a single step inside your apartment."

She thumbed his nipple then drew her attention to their surroundings and their mutual state of disarray. A victorious, albeit weary, smile touched her lips and she once again snuggled down against him. The dark silk of her hair spilling over his chest.

"I'll give you everything in the divorce if you don't make me move from this spot."

Ryan collected the long strands and smoothed them down her back.

"No dice. After being used to within an inch of my life, I deserve a bed..." Thinking of the way she'd been on him before he'd even managed to kick the door closed, he tsked, "And you do too."

Reluctantly, he shifted, separating their bodies as he gathered Claire into his arms and then carried her toward the back of the apartment. There was a single bedroom with a queen-size bed tucked off to one side. His feet would be hanging off the end tonight, but with Claire in his arms, it wouldn't matter.

Gently he stripped her bare and tucked her beneath the thick duvet, crawling in beside her. She wiggled into his hold, sighing against his hand as their bodies pressed together. She'd be asleep in seconds, but he needed her coherent just a little longer.

His mouth brushed the smooth curve of her bare shoulder. "Claire."

She sighed again. Her breath slowing, growing heavier.

"Claire." A light nip. This one earning him a squeak and her full attention.

"What?" she snapped, trying to roll away from him. But he caught her hip with his hand and pulled her back to him, holding her close.

"No more dates with other guys. Just so we're clear. Not until we're done."

She stilled in his arms, then after a beat, "No more dates."

CHAPTER SIXTEEN

CLAIRE buckled her belt at her waist and adjusted the hang of her houndstooth skirt in the mirror, all the while aware of Ryan watching from the bed behind her. She'd intentionally chosen an outfit that, though stylish and contemporary, wasn't particularly sexy. With all the days she'd missed from work recently, she knew it was going to be another busy day. The last thing she needed—as much as she might enjoy it—was to be hours late courtesy of Ryan liking the way something split at her knee.

Only, feeling the hot lick of his gaze trailing over the backs of her thighs, she wasn't sure the skirt had done the job. And she hadn't even risked the boots yet, intending to carry the stacked-heel footwear to the front door before slipping them on and making a dash for the nearest cab. So much for that.

"I need to get to work," she warned, shooting a chiding glance over her shoulder. "I can get away with a half day, probably. Maybe leaving by three?"

It would hurt, but the man had shown up, as if she'd conjured him out of thin air. The least she could do was manage a few extra hours for him.

Leaning back against the headrest, he crossed his arms over his chest and grinned. "How about I come with you. I'll set up in your office. Believe me when I tell you I've got plenty to do."

She fumbled her necklace, a clunky brass chain adorned with crocheted cherries and rhinestone-encrusted leaves. "The whole day?"

"Sure." He hopped off the bed, coming up behind to catch the clasp, waiting as he used to for her to lift her hair clear. "If you don't think it would be too much distraction."

A hot open mouthed kiss at her nape sent a shiver coursing through her and her senses reeling.

"I'll promise to be good."

God, he was always good. The man could be good in the backseat of a Volkswagen Bug. Good wasn't the problem. Nor the distraction.

It was him.

Inside her gallery. Penetrating her last refuge.

She wanted to hold out. Protect it. Only deep down, she knew he'd infiltrated that sanctuary weeks ago. His touch haunting her memories, the question of when she'd see him next dominating her thoughts.

Strong hands closed over her shoulders as he turned her to face him. Playing with the red bobble at the base of her throat, he smiled wolfishly. "Cherries. My favorite."

Her gaze shot the length of him. Open white oxford and dark-rinse jeans. No shoes.

Her favorite, too.

Catching her hand where it had drifted to the hard plane of his belly, Ryan rubbed a thumb across the rise of each knuckle. "So, what do you say? Work date?"

"Yes." Resisting Ryan just wasn't part of her makeup.

Claire was in her element. Now he understood. The gallery was something she'd built to be a part of her, rather than simply a place where she worked. Something she did.

They'd walked through the doors that morning and it was

as if the space breathed her in, drawing her away from him in a way he hadn't expected. Couldn't compete with.

Not that he wanted to. Not really.

He just hadn't been prepared for her move away from him so abruptly. Both physically and mentally.

He should have though. At least in the physical regard. The relationship hadn't been publicized. They'd been selective in their outings and quiet about the affair in general. New York had been a risk, but one Ryan ultimately had been willing to take.

And if he were totally honest with himself, he'd been curious about her life here. He'd wanted to see the home she'd made without him. Wanted to touch the part of her that hadn't existed when they'd been together. But of course that meant *touching her* in public was out of the question.

At the gallery, Claire garnered the same "look all you want, but hands off" treatment as the works of art adorning her walls. So they'd stood three feet apart. And he'd tamped down that recurring impulse to lay a proprietary arm across her shoulders or hand over the curve at her waist.

There had been a few questioning stares from both patrons and staff alike, but Sally, Claire's competent assistant, had stepped in, deftly diverting the attention as they'd made their way back to Claire's office. And if he'd thought to get her on top of her desk or against the door in there, he'd been sorely mistaken. Claire was a workhorse with an open-door policy. One that she wasn't modifying for him.

They worked across the desk from one another through most of the morning. Claire stepping out from time to time and then settling back to look through another prospective artist's work or answer calls from her clients.

Ryan wasn't accustomed to sharing an office, but it had worked out and by early afternoon he was ready for a break.

Claire was just wrapping a call when he rounded her desk and, miraculously finding a square of open space, rested one hip atop the surface. It wasn't provocative or overly presumptuous, but Claire's gaze invariably shot to the door as she rolled her chair back a few inches. Only, Ryan had been good all day, and he didn't want her getting away from him quite so quickly. Reaching out easily enough, he grabbed her seat back, holding her trapped momentarily captive.

"Think you've accomplished enough to justify breaking for lunch?"

Her gaze roved over the desktop as she openly considered. Then, blinking up at him, "Something quick?"

"No roach-coach, if that's what you mean." He valued her life too much to risk it on lunch off the back of a truck.

When she continued to hesitate, he briefly caught her chin before pulling back his hold. If he wasn't careful, he'd be stroking his thumb across her lips and slipping his hand around the back of her neck. And it would only get better from there.

So he was being careful. Damn it.

"Even if someone spots us together at a restaurant. So what? I could be a client."

She leaned back into her chair. "Or you could be my husband. If my name weren't Brady it would be different. But all it would take is one person putting Brady and Brady together, getting curious and— Honestly, I don't know exactly how I feel about what we're doing, myself. I'm just not ready to answer questions for anyone else."

"Claire!" The enthusiastic squeal sounded from the doorway, followed immediately by a small body, smelling distinctly of chorine, barreling into the office. "I told you she'd be here!"

"Corbin, you need to knock first… Sorry, Claire" came the patiently chiding voice of a woman a few paces back.

Ryan stepped clear of the desk and out of the fray just as Corbin crashed into Claire's chair.

"Hi, Jane. How's it going, little man?" she asked, laughing even as she waved off the mother's apologetic frown.

"Good." The boy grabbed his belt, hitching his jeans to rib height as he readied his response. "We watched *Clone Wars* this morning and I had swimming and you said my painting was gonna be ready on Saturday, so I told Mom we *needed* to come."

Ryan watched as Claire's brows incrementally rose with each fact bulleted off, emphasizing to the little tyke that she was following his every word. And was duly impressed as well. Her entire posture relaxed around this family and Ryan wondered who they were to her. And if she intended to simply pretend he wasn't there rather than acknowledge to her friends who he was.

Apparently that was exactly what she intended, as evidenced when she rose from her chair and began ushering the lot of them toward the door. "What do you say we head back to the studio and check it out?"

Studio? Was this some child prodigy? The boy didn't have the gloomy gaunt intensity he would have figured to go along with that kind of youthful creative genius, but maybe he'd just watched too much TV. There was no law that said well-fed, happy kids couldn't paint.

Jane shot him a nervous glance and began shaking her head in protest. "I don't want to interrupt your meeting…"

Claire, obviously seeing no way around it, set her shoulders and faced Ryan with a strained smile. "No, this is nothing. Nothing to interrupt. *Totally* nothing."

He wanted to laugh.

Way to sell it, Claire. She couldn't lie to save her life. Never could.

"I'm Ryan," he said, offering his hand for a quick shake.

Then, unable to resist a poke at Claire, added, "Nothing, Ryan."

Jane giggled and Corbin twisted up his face with pained urgency. *"Come on."*

Claire, all too happy to accommodate, led the way down a back hall to a room he hadn't been shown on the introductory tour. A brightly lit studio stocked with children's-size easels, clotheslines strung with pictures and bin upon bin of colorful supplies stacked low against the walls.

Corbin, who didn't seem to walk anywhere, skidded across the open floor to a drying rack where he retrieved his latest masterpiece, gently displaying it for their approval.

Claire crouched in front of him, talking quietly about his use of color and negative space. The kid couldn't be seven, but he nodded along with everything she said, making sure his mother fully appreciated the technique. Then, noting an audience member fallen out of the fold, Corbin hiked up his belt again and strode over to Ryan, thrusting the painting up at him.

"It's the blue park behind my house."

"I like it." There was plenty of blue. And surprisingly enough detail to back up the park claim. Though this kid's work definitely wasn't the next exhibit in the gallery's West Hall.

"Do you see the sandbox?"

Obviously a cursory examination wasn't going to do it. And the boy was so proud, really—what would a few minutes' praise cost him?

Crouching as he'd seen Claire do, he looked more closely. Picked out as many recognizable details as he could. Asked questions and warmed to the critique as their exchange continued.

And then he was laughing with this little boy whose antics

were peculiar and irresistible all at once. Charmed by his exuberance and glee.

It was funny. Ryan had always liked kids—thought he'd have a big brood of them himself one day. But it hadn't worked out that way, and after Claire left he'd found it easier to steer clear of domesticity as it happened around him than to deal with it. It hadn't been difficult. For the most part, his interactions tended toward the professional. He worked. A lot. And the people he played with worked a lot, too. It was their common interest, so to speak. As an only child himself, there weren't any nieces or nephews to be tossing around either. So he'd effectively distanced himself from moments like this one.

But, as devastated and broken as she'd been by their loss, somehow Claire had not. It made him happy to learn that she'd made room for children in this life she'd constructed for herself, even if they weren't her own.

Their own.

He swallowed, taking another look at the boy who huddled against him. Saw the dark mop of straight hair, the bright blue eyes, and olive skin, and wondered if this was what Andrew might have looked like. If their child would have been bursting with so much energy that his little feet couldn't stop moving even when he'd been trying so hard to stand still. If he'd like to paint pictures for his mother, who had wanted him so badly, and tell his daddy about the bus ride to school and the bug that got into the library.

And then he felt it. That tiny weight in his hand that was the end of everything he'd loved, all the plans they'd made. His baby so small, so young, that he'd never had a chance.

For a moment the sense of loss was so fresh, so sharp, it cut through him like a knife. Reminding him why he'd worked so hard not to think about those old dreams at all. He needed to get out of there. Needed to breathe—something. But as he straightened, he caught sight of Claire. Stricken. Staring at him.

At them.

CHAPTER SEVENTEEN

SHE'D followed his thoughts. Or found her own path to the same end. But either way, in that moment they were together. United in the loss that had eviscerated their lives.

He wanted to run. To get away. To lose himself in anything that would blot that decade-old heartache from his memory.

This was what he hadn't wanted.

Only then, Corbin darted around a small table, hurtling himself at his mother's knees, chirping about his next painting and how many days was it until the next workshop and what were they having for dinner.

Claire laughed—the sorrow in her eyes miraculously replaced by mirth—and reached out to rub the boy's head. "Next week. You're going to be here, right?"

"Uh-huh," came the vigorous reply, and a nod so big it set him back a pace.

Jane took her son's hand with a soft chuckle, guiding Corbin out of the studio behind her.

Ryan rubbed a hand across the back of his neck, then crossed his arms, watching Claire. She'd recovered quickly, but he'd seen it. The heartbreak that had been the end of their marriage. The end of who she'd been to him, to herself, and the predecessor to who she'd become. "You want to talk about it?"

She shook her head, busying herself with a pile of Conté

crayons. "It was you. Seeing you with that little boy." Her eyes closed, her head angling a degree, as though she was mentally replaying the moment. "Laughing and carrying on. And then you looked at him. *Really* looked at him… And I saw it."

Ryan crossed the room, pulling her into his arms, anyone walking past the studio be damned. She didn't stiffen or pull away, but leaned into him. Let him hold her and pretend he had some comfort to offer.

As though he wasn't years too late, and a lifetime together too short.

"You looked at your hands like he was still there. And—" she swallowed, pulling in a shaky breath where her head rested against his chest "—it just caught me off guard."

"Yeah, me too," he breathed into her hair, stroking a hand down her back as much to soothe as to keep her in his arms. Keep her close enough that she couldn't see his face. Read the rough emotion that was tearing at him from the inside out.

Only, somehow she didn't need to see him to know. "Ryan?"

And right then, he just didn't have it in him to try to hide the truth that was eating at him. Had been eating at him for nine years. "I didn't do enough."

Claire pulled back, shocked by the admission. "What are you talking about? There was nothing we could do. The doctors explained, the cyst ruptured before anyone knew it was there—"

"After that, Claire." He closed his eyes and shook his head. "When you couldn't heal your heart, and I couldn't figure out what you needed, I gave up. You might have said the words, but I let you go. Too easily."

Her heart began a slow pound that seemed to reverberate through every cell in her body. "What are you saying?"

"I saw the opportunity and I wanted it. I wanted out. I wanted to be something other than the guy who'd let his wife down when she needed him to be there for her. Who couldn't hurt deeply enough to connect anymore. Who worked himself into oblivion so he didn't have to come home and see the heartbreak scattered around him. I made it easy for you to leave because I'd already found a way to be gone." Abruptly Ryan turned away, crossed to a worktable, where he braced his arms wide and let his head hang forward. "What kind of husband does that?"

She blinked back the tears she couldn't afford to shed, relieved in that moment to have Ryan's back. She knew the answer, but couldn't voice the words without revealing the depth of hurt they caused.

The kind of husband who'd married his wife for the sake of a child lost before he'd ever had the chance to live.

Yes, they'd been in love. In lust. In everything a couple of kids—and at eighteen and twenty-two that's what they'd been—could be. But they'd married because she was pregnant. If not for that, chances were their romance would have died out on its own within a year or two. They'd have gone their separate ways. Led their separate lives. And done it without the burden of a past neither wanted to face, tainting every interaction that followed.

Ryan had done the honorable thing, and he'd done it without a moment's hesitation or a single word of prompting. And after they lost Andrew, yes, he took refuge in his work. *But he hadn't left.*

"You did everything I let you. More. You might have felt some relief when I left, but how could you not? The way I treated you…" Her lips pressed together as she sought the strength to say the words she'd owed him for too long. "It wasn't right. I was angry, Ryan. Angry at the injustice of it all. Angry at my parents for abandoning me when I needed them the most."

"Your parents were self-absorbed jerks without a clue what

love or commitment or responsibility meant. They deserved every bit of your anger." He bit off each word, his rage sounding as fresh as it had nearly ten years before.

"I know. But those feelings weren't something I'd ever had to deal with before. I was so spoiled. And if I were just angry at them, it would have been one thing…but I wasn't."

"You were angry with me." He'd known it. Said the words without any trace of condemnation, which made it all the worse.

"Yes." She nodded, unable to look him in the eyes as she laid open the wound of their past. "For not breaking. For being stronger than I was and being able to go on with your life. Your job…for having something left, when I felt like I had nothing."

"Nothing," he echoed with a hollow resignation that pained her all the more.

"All I could see was that you'd married me because I was pregnant. And I'd lost our baby. And—"

"And, what, you thought I was like your parents? That you somehow hadn't kept up your end of the bargain? *I loved you.*"

"I ruined our lives! If I couldn't stop resenting myself, blaming myself, how could you?"

His hands clamped tight around her shoulders as he shook. "What was there to blame?"

"I was terrible to you, Ryan. When you tried to help me, I wouldn't even talk to you. I wouldn't look at you. Touch you."

"Claire, your life went to hell in a matter of months. You were eighteen. Yes, you pushed me away. But I *let* you. And then I let you go."

"When I *needed* you to. You did."

"God, you make it sound like some kind of a gift instead of a failure."

"It was a gift. I needed to make my own life and I needed to let you have yours. And because of your support, I was able to."

He stared hard into her eyes as though he couldn't believe what she was saying. As if he knew there was something more.

And he was right. But there was only one more part that she could give him.

"I *loved* you," she whispered, the old words ragged with emotion and the painful need to be renewed. But that wasn't what this was about. What was happening between them now, more than the nights in each other's arms, was closure. "I would have given *anything* for the life we almost had together, Ryan. I mourned the loss of it, like I mourned Andrew. But some things just aren't meant to be."

Ryan's arms slid around her back, pulling her against him completely. And for once, it felt as though she was lending as much strength as she took.

CHAPTER EIGHTEEN

CLAIRE woke to the muted light of a nightside lamp and Ryan's hand coasting across her belly. Drifting from the rise of one pelvic bone to the other. Brushing lightly over the bare skin with a touch so gentle it almost wasn't there. His broad shoulders tensed as he supported his weight on one elbow, leaning close to follow the progress of his hand with his eyes.

Searching.

He didn't realize she was awake.

"There aren't any," she said, her whisper a roar against the quiet of night.

Ryan turned to meet her eyes, steady, unapologetic, his palm flattening over her stomach.

"Stretch marks. That's what you're looking for, right?"

"I just wondered. I hadn't noticed before, but..."

But they weren't generally the kind of thing a man looked for while in the throes of passion.

She'd looked for them though. Over the years, searching for any trace of the silvery lines that served as the badges of motherhood, wondering if somehow she'd missed just one. "No."

"You never got very big."

"That and youth. Within a year, you couldn't tell I'd ever been pregnant."

Ryan nodded, but the corners of his mouth had pulled into

a frown. As if he knew she hadn't considered the evidence of their lost child being erased from her body any kind of gift at all.

Dropping a tender kiss to the sunken plane of her abdomen, Ryan closed his eyes and then moved up the bed. Their bodies realigned back to front, coming to rest together in that perfect fit of hard and soft, dips and curves, valleys and swells.

She'd slept alone for so many years. It was hard to believe how quickly they'd fallen into the comfort of that old tangle of limbs. But within seconds of settling into his loose hold, she was drifting. Body disconnecting from mind. Reality blurring around the edges until—

"Why don't you have a family?"

She might have mistaken the unexpected question as a by-product of her imagination, if not for the way the words rumbled against her back and burrowed through her hair.

Eyes blinking open, she was instantly alert. Frozen in place by the fear of a conversation she wasn't prepared to have. Not with Ryan. Not tonight. Not ever.

Maybe if she simply didn't respond, if she lay still, pretending she'd already passed into sleep, Ryan would do the same. Only, he must have felt her react to his words, because the arm that had draped across her torso pulled back, allowing him to caress her hip and thigh with a few soothing strokes.

"I know what you told me about your…response to other men over the years. But kids…it's different."

She knew what he was saying, of course. A woman didn't have to feel passion to get pregnant. Hell, she didn't even need a husband. But passion had only been part of the problem. And admitting that much to Ryan had been hard enough.

"It's late," she murmured against the pillow in the hopes the down would filter the strained edge to her voice. "You've got an early flight out tomorrow."

"I'll sleep on the plane. You sleep in here." A moment

passed, long enough that she could all but see the contemplation taking place in his mind. He'd caught on to her resistance. And now he was wondering why. The only question was how he'd come back at her.

"You're keeping something from me."

Directly, then.

No question. No subtle prompting. Just a statement of fact. One she would deny.

"I don't know what you're talking about," she answered on a controlled sigh, going for dismissive fatigue.

Ryan's fingers curled over her hip, turning her to her back so he could see her face. So she didn't have anywhere to hide.

"Claire." He said her name like a judgment. Like that single word gave him access to all the secrets of her soul. And resentment began a low simmer throughout her veins.

"You aren't my husband anymore. Just because we're sharing a bed doesn't mean you have a right to my every private thought."

His jaw clenched and those gently probing eyes went hard above her, boring into her then with unyielding determination. "I may not have been your husband for the last nine years, but I sure as hell am tonight."

Her body went rigid beneath him. The claim slicing through her like a blade.

"You think you get to pick and choose, Ryan? Tonight you're my husband but tomorrow you're not? Is that how it works?"

A muttered curse pushed through his teeth. "I don't know how it works. I just know that tonight, we're more than two people having an affair. And I know that for some reason, you'd rather pick a fight than be straight with me. Claire, after everything we've been through today, what is this?"

"It's me being tired and telling you to back off."

She didn't like the contrast of their positions—she on her back, Ryan looming above her—but if she leveled the field and sat up, it would be conceding to a conversation she didn't want to have. She'd rather he look down at her.

"Back off?" he snapped, leaning in closer, anger hardening the cut of his features. "I'm leaving in six hours, how far is it you want me to go?"

"I don't know, how far is it going to take?"

He stared at her a long moment and she wondered if he'd simply roll off the bed and leave. If she could stand to watch him go, simply so she could hold on to this last secret. But then his focus narrowed and an icy chill slid over her spine.

"I asked you about a family because it's clear how much you love kids."

Claire shrank back into the mattress, the kick of fight lost as quickly as it had come. Ryan wasn't going to let her push him away, distract him with her temper, or manipulate her way out of this corner she'd found herself in.

"And now you're afraid to tell me what's so wrong with what I asked."

That fast, he'd figured it out. Not just that she didn't want to talk about it, but that she was *afraid to talk to him* about it. He wouldn't give it up now. No way. She might as well tell him, maybe if she'd just told him from the beginning, instead of trying to keep the truth buried, the whole thing would have amounted to nothing. But she hadn't and now Ryan wouldn't let it go.

"I suppose you could have looked into artificial insemination."

Her eyes widened at his first guess and he shrugged that suggestion off. "Okay, not that. Or maybe you could have—"

"No, I couldn't," she cut in, unwilling to wait as Ryan systematically narrowed the possibilities until only one remained.

"Whatever you're about to say, Ryan, I couldn't have. I can't get pregnant."

Moments ago, the body braced above her had been immovable, if for no other reason than Ryan's will. But now it seemed to have set in stone. Breath arrested, eyes unseeing, all signs of life frozen in that instant of understanding.

Then, "But the doctors said we would be able to...."

We. She hadn't thought it possible, but somehow that single word made it all the worse.

"It happened later. Another ruptured cyst..." She drew a steadying breath and shrugged in quiet acceptance of the hand she'd been dealt. "There were complications."

At complications, Ryan's brow drew down. "How serious?"

"I was in the hospital for a few days." Then aiming for a little levity, she added, "But, obviously, you can see I recovered."

He didn't crack a smile or so much as blink. But then there really wasn't much to laugh about. "You could have called. I would have been there for you."

She knew. "I didn't want you to worry. Or feel sorry for me."

"Did you have someone there? Sally?"

Claire slid back against the headboard to sit, hiding her uneasy squirm beneath the purpose of action.

"I wasn't alone." It was truth without full disclosure. She hadn't met Sally for another year, but that time frame would be too telling, so she left her answer there.

Only, the dodge wasn't subtle enough.

"But not with Sally."

Damn it. "No."

Turning eyes on her that were somehow both bleak and condemning all at once, he ground out his demand. "How long ago?"

Desperately she looked away, grasping for any reprieve

that would protect them both. But then he had her shoulders in his grip. "How long? And don't even think about lying to me, Claire. I'll see it in your face and I'll have the answer on my own in less than twenty-four hours. So tell me."

And he would.

Her shoulders sagged in defeat and the hold that had trapped her only seconds ago now held her up.

"Six years ago. New York."

His features contorted, twisting into an agonizing mask of pain. "Before."

No question of what he meant. Before she'd called to tell him she wasn't coming back.

She couldn't bear to look at him. "Yes."

"What did you wait then?" he demanded, the bitter accusation of his words turning her stomach and burning her eyes. "A week, a month, before deciding the rest of our lives for us?"

"That isn't fair," she gasped. "Our marriage was over already. You know it was."

And with that, the last tether on his control snapped. Face red, eyes blazing, he stabbed a damning finger at the air between them. "It wasn't over until you made that call!"

The force of his words hit like a blast to her heart. They hurt and stunned, but she wouldn't back down because she knew what she'd done had been right. Ryan would never have given up on them, no matter how much he might have wanted or needed to. It wasn't who he was. How he worked. And that's why she hadn't told him what happened. She couldn't stand for his sense of obligation to keep him with her, when he deserved to have more.

"I wanted you to have a life."

"Damn it, Claire." He stared at her as if he couldn't believe she'd missed the point. *"I had one."*

"No. Not with me." Before they'd lost their baby, yes. But not after. Not the way she'd become.

Swiping at her tears with the back of her wrist, she offered her only defense. "I wanted you to have more."

Raking a hand through his hair, Ryan's focus dropped to her belly before returning to her eyes. "More than you could give me."

What else was there to say? "Yes."

Closing her eyes, she rested her face against her knees she'd tucked up against her and let the soft cotton sheet absorb the tears she couldn't stop from falling.

The mattress shifted, and then Ryan's arms were there, pulling her into his chest as he laid them back, tucking her head beneath his chin.

Moments passed as they lay together in the dark, awake but unspeaking.

Then Ryan's hand stroked over her shoulder as his mouth pressed into her hair.

"Okay. So now I know."

Shouldering the strap of his carry-on, Ryan watched as Claire curled into herself beneath the blankets he'd pulled over her, a troubled furrow pinching her brow even as she slept. They'd lain awake most of the night, but somewhere around five she'd finally relaxed against him, her breathing falling into the steady rhythm of sleep. Little more than an hour later, he couldn't bring himself to wake her as he gathered the few things he'd brought for the two-night stay.

Now it was time to leave and he still couldn't go to her. Wouldn't risk a goodbye kiss and the chance of her sleep-hazed vulnerability pulling him into those bottomless blues as she asked the inevitable question.

What next?

Maybe it was cowardice. But he didn't know what to say.

Didn't even know how to begin sorting through the mess they'd made of something that was supposed to have been so simple.

He'd thought he knew what happened to their life, their marriage. Had come to terms with the loss and failures as he'd perceived them, that that final call had been the result of Claire learning she was happier without him. That the rift opened when they'd lost their baby had simply grown too wide to risk crossing.

That she'd grown out of loving him.

But that's not how it had been.

She could have been wondering if a future together was possible. If she'd found enough of herself to try to build something new. She could have been ready to board a plane and come home. But he'd never know now. Not for sure.

The only thing he could be sure of was that Claire had wanted more for him than she'd believed she could offer. And whatever she'd been thinking prior to that hospital stay had ceased to matter by the time she left. Because by then she'd made her decision to do the right thing for him.

Another damn sacrifice.

It was almost laughable.

How many times had he thought over the last couple of months how surprisingly attractive this tough, painfully independent version of Claire was. Wondered when all that strength had been forged.

Well, now he knew.

Six years ago. In the most selfish act of generosity he could imagine.

The old rage burned through him. That same suffocating sense of helpless impotence that had driven him in every decision he'd made since he was eight years old and just beginning to understand the kinds of sacrifices his mother was making to provide the life she wanted him to have. No life of her own.

He'd done everything he could to ease her burdens. Busted his ass to make grades, to earn scholarships. Hustling every opportunity he could find. In the end he realized they'd done it together. His success had been her dream, her reward. And at last he'd been able to ease her burdens.

But that wasn't the case with Claire. She hadn't been protecting a helpless child.

He was a man. He was her husband. And instead of letting him be there for her, she'd hidden the truth from him. Once again refusing to trust him with information he had a right to. Refusing to give him a say in the life they'd vowed to spend together.

Ryan turned from the soft temptation of Claire's bed and headed down the hall, the hardwood echoing its protest with his every step. At the front door, he heard his name. A groggy, muffled inquiry. Quietly, he closed the door, set to lock, behind him.

She hadn't given him a choice or even an honest explanation about what happened to their life.

And now, he didn't know if he could forgive her.

CHAPTER NINETEEN

IT was early dawn and surfers bobbed like black dots across the water's surface, waiting to catch their wave. Ryan wanted to be out there with them. One with the ocean. Fluid in body and mind. At peace with the world around him.

Not today though.

Nothing gelled. Nothing fit or flowed or felt right and hadn't since he'd left Claire the day before. He'd been banking on the demands of the job—conference calls and a backlog of work that was the result of all the time he'd been making for Claire—to keep his head clear. But it hadn't worked and Claire had lingered at the edge of most every thought.

He'd planned to call her today though. To make sure she was okay and come to some decisions about their future.

That's what he'd planned before the predawn call from his Boston-based assistant.

Now it was barely five-thirty and already he'd spent half an hour on the phone. The news wasn't good. And the timing couldn't be worse.

"Look, Denis, I haven't talked to Dahlia in months." And he was kicking himself, hard, for not having followed up with her after that last missed call. "What exactly do we know?"

Papers shuffled from across the country, the noise somehow reassuring within the waiting silence currently surrounding Ryan. "Nothing more than I've already told you. It's tabloid

fodder. She declined wine with dinner and made a couple suggestive statements to the press. But this is Dahlia we're talking
about. She's always stirring up something for publicity."

Ryan didn't need to be reminded, having been a part of her
publicity plan on and off for the better part of a year. Rubbing
a hand across the tightening muscles of his neck, he closed
his eyes. "You said she's in L.A.?"

"Yes, they've been shooting this week."

"Okay, I'll get in touch with Dahlia myself. Clear my morning through…hell, make it three this afternoon."

Hanging up, Ryan let his head fall back against the chair.
A pregnancy. Of all the damn things in the world, it had to be
that. It wasn't likely true, and even less that the baby would
be his…but there was the possibility. He needed answers and
he needed them fast. Depending on what Dahlia said, any
decision about a future with Claire might not be his to make.
Claire had demonstrated that already.

Ryan set his napkin aside. "You're positive?"

Laughter bubbled free of Dahlia Dawson's full, internation-
ally recognizable smile as amusement lit her eyes. "Of course
I'm sure. Do you really think I wouldn't know who'd gotten
me pregnant?"

He hadn't known what to think, but relief washed over him
that Dahlia was confident she did.

Leaning into him, she caught his face in the cup of her
palm. Outwardly the gesture was intimate tenderness, but
inwardly it was like so much with Dahlia. Staged.

He hadn't minded the occasional lack of authenticity when
they'd been dating. In fact, at times, it more than suited his
needs. He'd had the soft press of a stunning woman at his side,
the charming company and dazzling conversation, without
any actual risk of a messy entanglement.

Sure, there had been plenty of unscripted time too. Behind

closed doors, she relaxed into who she really was. Gave up the pretense and posing. Mostly. But they'd never connected to the point where all boundaries could be dropped.

There had been just enough between them to make a casual relationship go the distance. It was only when *casual* stopped working and Dahlia began to want something that went deeper than he'd been able to offer, they went their separate ways. He had hurt her. But not the way he would have if they'd continued.

Dahlia was better for it. Beneath the show of calculated motions and measured laughter, she was lit with a glow from within. One that couldn't be manufactured. "You're happy now?"

The smile that split her face in that moment was one he'd never seen before. It was genuine, carrying emotion too great to be contained. Her gaze dipped to the slight swell of her belly, pushing his thoughts to Claire and the ache that had settled deep in the middle of his chest.

"I am."

Damn, that was good to know. It's what he'd wanted for her. "You deserve it, sweetheart."

"Goodbye, Ryan."

Taking her hand from his cheek, he gave it a gentle squeeze.

Walking from the restaurant, the light reprieve of relief and satisfaction evaporated and a heavy weight settled over his shoulders. He needed to call Claire.

Even though the anger hadn't ebbed, his thoughts hadn't particularly cleared, he needed to hear her voice.

Only, a call from the office was already coming through.

"We've got a problem with the Lake deal," was Denis's efficient greeting. "I'm holding a conference call for you now."

The Lake deal again. Details dropped into place as he

mentally shifted focus, his stride lengthening as he headed for his car. "What have you got for me?"

Denis delivered the points of update in bulletlike fashion, leaving Ryan wondering if the deal he'd been working for the last six months could be resuscitated after apparently being shot to hell in the last day. But already his mind was spinning toward solutions, reevaluating the risk to reward and settling on the answer. Yes.

Calling Claire was out. Thirty seconds to tell her he didn't have time wouldn't be doing either of them any favors. But without even a goodbye he had to do something.

"Denis, shoot an email to Claire letting her know I'm going to be tied up with this, probably through the night. I'll call her when I have a chance." One more day might give him the perspective he needed to make some decisions. For now, though, he needed one hundred percent of his focus to salvage this deal. "Okay, conference me in."

Claire blinked at the celebrity headline, let her focus slip to the photo beneath.

Ryan gazing tenderly into the elated face of Dahlia Dawson, who in turn cupped his strong jaw with her palm. It was an intimate moment between two people caught unawares by the press. Two people making plans for a future.

WEDDING IN THE WORKS FOR EXPECTANT PARENTS BRADY AND DAWSON

She closed her eyes, as if that would be enough to make her forget. Somehow make it less real.

It wasn't fair. It wasn't right.

Three nights ago Ryan had been in her bed. Holding her against his heart and telling her that, if only for that night, he was her husband again. It hardly seemed possible that as he'd searched her body for signs of the child they'd lost, another was already growing within Dahlia's womb.

Nausea roiled within her. She'd never had a chance.

She'd been bound for heartbreak from that first day in Rome.

No, that wasn't right. It could have been different. She might have been able to escape with minimal damage… if she'd remembered what they were engaging in was only an affair. If she hadn't begun to wonder about more…think maybe, this time, there was enough right—

She'd been an idiot.

Holding up the paper she forced herself to see reality.

Ryan looked happy. The smile on his face was relaxed. Satisfied. As though he had exactly what he wanted.

A child. *His child.*

He'd made such a great show of avoiding commitment all these years—but maybe, like her, he'd been telling himself the things he couldn't have were things he didn't want.

Memories of their past slipped like filmy overlays to the present. To another pregnancy. Another lifetime.

God, he'd been so happy. Stunned for all of a quarter of a second when she'd told him the news. She'd been terrified—so afraid of what he'd say, what he'd want.

What he wouldn't want.

To that point everything between them had been perfect. She'd believed he loved her. But they'd only been together for a matter of months and a pregnancy could change everything.

It had changed everything. First in the most incredible way and then in the most devastating. Within days she'd lost her parents, within months she'd lost Andrew, and within a year Ryan. But in those initial moments, it had been bliss. Ryan's frozen expression cracking into the widest of grins as he pulled her into his arms, off her feet, and spun her around laughing.

He'd told her it hadn't been the way he'd planned it, but he'd always seen a family as part of his life, he'd just thought he'd have to wait. He saw her pregnancy as the gift he got to open before Christmas morning. And then he'd asked her to marry him.

Now, pressure bit at her eyes, tightened her throat around a well of emotion too great to swallow down. Ryan didn't have to wait anymore for the gift so cruelly snatched back from his fingers. A gift Claire could never give him.

Praying to God this child was born without a single complication, she fisted her hand and jammed it against her lips, trying to stifle the sound of choked despair.

The phone was ringing again. Sally, not Ryan.

She'd have to pick up eventually, but today there was only one call she was going to take. The one from Ryan where he told her they were over and this divorce and settlement they'd been dragging their feet on would need to be resolved in short order.

The absence of that call meant only one thing. He didn't know about the article. The man's protective drive toward her bordered on obsessive-compulsive disorder.

Or at least it had.

But that would inevitably change with this reversal of roles too.

Dahlia would become his wife. The woman who carried his baby. And if he'd been protective of Claire— A weak laugh escaped her, slipping through her fingers and echoing down the empty hall where she'd slumped against the wall upon opening the morning paper—Dahlia would be lucky if he let her leave the house encased in Bubble Wrap.

Whereas Claire...well, he'd always care about her, but she had become that other woman with whom "it was over."

Over. The word shifted restlessly in her mind, unwilling to settle or take root.

But denial wouldn't change the fact that it was where they had been heading from the first.

Regardless of the detours made along the way, that final destination should never have been in question. Claire should never have allowed herself to get in so deep. It had been stupid and careless to leave herself open to this kind of vulnerability when, in truth, Ryan had never given her one word of encouragement that the relationship would go anywhere but to divorce.

What kind of fool was she that after all the years it had taken to climb out of that dark abyss, the moment she was finally free she threw herself down right back at the ledge by slipping into love with the man who'd told her flat out the limit on what he could offer.

She'd willingly exposed that most tender part of her heart again, and look where it left her. Staring down into those same dark depths.

She wouldn't give in. Not this time.

CHAPTER TWENTY

RYAN disconnected the call and contemplated giving in to his body's immediate demand for sleep. But after eighteen hours and four back-to-back conferences calls tying him to his desk, he couldn't tolerate another minute within the confines of an office that had gone as stale as the coffee he'd given up on a handful of hours before.

Rubbing the top of his head, he walked into the main hall only half registering the increase in stares and decrease in chatter as he cut past a bank of cubes on his way to the small apartment he kept at the far end of the suite of offices. It wasn't luxurious, but it was stocked with a few changes of clothing, toiletries and enough nonperishable food to get him through.

Cranking the tap in the shower with one hand, he pulled at his tie with the other. Shower. Shave. New suit.

Sleep could wait until tonight. A call to Claire couldn't though. She'd stayed with him through all the hours of wrestling this deal back on track. Thoughts of her laughter as haunting as his name on her lips that last morning.

He shouldn't have left without a goodbye.

His phone sounded with another call from Denis. Toeing off his shoes, he answered, "Damn, you're relentless, man. Not even ten minutes."

A somewhat strained laugh was followed by the clearing of

Denis's throat, and instantly Ryan shook off the punch-drunk haze. "What's going on?"

"You made the papers this morning. I didn't see it until just now, but you're not going to like it."

Steam beckoned from the waiting shower. Ryan let out a heavy breath, stalked into the bathroom and shut it off. "Which paper?"

"All of them."

"Pick up!"

Another droning ring and Ryan's knuckles whitened over the phone in his grasp. Briefcase and jacket stuffed under his arm, he tore across the office lobby, ignoring the stares of those who'd recognized him from the morning news.

He'd gone through to voice mail on her cell phone, gotten the run-around from the gallery, was disconnected when he'd tried to get Sally on the line, and now Claire wasn't answering at home either.

She'd seen the story. No chance she'd missed it. Every network across the country was reporting on Dahlia Dawson's pregnancy and impending nuptials—both confirmed by her PR manager. Unfortunately no clarification had been made re the groom's identity, which meant Claire had spent the better part of the day with every reason to believe it was true.

Voice mail again.

Damn it! His gut knotted at the sound of her recorded voice directing him to leave a message.

Immediately he hung up and dialed again, shoving out the lobby doors.

One ring. His car was idling, ready to go.

Another. Stuffing a bill into the valet's hand, he levered into the driver's seat and slipped the hands-free device over his ear.

"Hello," she answered on the third, sounding weary and

worn. But after all the unanswered calls, her voice suddenly on the line jolted him like an electric shock.

"Thank God. Claire, it's not true."

Jerking the wheel, he cut into traffic as her breath, catching on a sob, cut into him.

"She's pregnant. I'd heard the rumor. It's why I met with her. To find out. But the baby isn't mine."

God, he needed to be there. Holding her as he explained. And then just holding her. Because he didn't want to be apart. It shouldn't have taken something like this to shake the sense loose in his head, but apparently it had. What happened in the past was behind them, and all that mattered was what happened now. How they chose to go forward from here.

But first making sure Claire was okay. That she understood. "I didn't know about the article. If I'd thought you'd find out like this, I swear I would have told you what I was doing. I just didn't want—" he broke off with a violent curse. He just hadn't wanted her to know about the rumor at all. Because he'd known it would hurt her. Scare her.

Possibly devastate her.

"Claire?" She should have said something by now. But maybe there was more to her silence than this rumor. Hell, he knew he had some making up to do. "Sweetheart, I'm sorry. I shouldn't have left without talking to you. I shouldn't have let this much time pass. Everything just got away from me, but I'm on my way to the airport now." He'd manage with the deal and the office and everything else. Somehow work around another screwup to the schedule. It didn't matter. Not like getting to Claire did. "I'll be there tonight. We'll talk then. About everything."

"No." Again, the soft whisper of her voice screamed at him from the silence that surrounded it.

The already tension-knotted muscles of his neck and shoulders ratcheted tighter, sending a shot of pain straight up to the base of his skull. "What do you mean no?"

The words whipped out of him faster than he could control. More harshly than he'd want her to hear. Almost as if they'd been poised, ready to go. As if, on some level, he'd already anticipated the need to use them.

A shaky breath sounded across the miles and the rest of Ryan's body tensed, bracing. And all he could think was, *Don't. Don't do this.*

"You don't need to come." Then, "You shouldn't."

Pulling over to the side of the road, Ryan's fist pounded against the wheel. His breath grating through his teeth.

Don't do it!

"This is more than I want, Ryan. More than I can handle."

"You're upset. This thing with Dahlia, with the press, it'll never happen again." The papers had been following him for years, but until now he'd never had a need to put a stop to it. For Claire he would though.

"Even before Dahlia, we let this go too far. I can't risk the kind of hurt…"

He knew she was scared. Understood how long it had taken her to come back from the emotional devastation she'd suffered nine years ago. But that wasn't what they were talking about. What they were doing together, this relationship still had boundaries, even if they'd slipped over the past days. They both still understood the limits were there. All she had to do was take a step back and—

"I *won't* risk it, Ryan."

A quiet calm sank into the center of his chest, drowning out the cold panic that had all but overtaken him mere moments ago. Staring out at the L.A. smog and congestion, he blew out a long breath. "So what now then?"

As if he didn't know.

"We cut our losses." The fragile quality of her voice had

been replaced by an impersonal clip. She was trying to turn it into business. "Let the lawyers wrap up the final asset division. And move on with our lives the way we were always supposed to."

"And that's it?"

"No." He could hear her hesitation, but knew better than to think she'd changed her mind. Knew from experience. "Thank you for letting me know about Dahlia... And, I'm sorry."

Disgusted, Ryan pulled the phone extension from his ear and tossed it to the empty seat beside him. He didn't need to ask. She was sorry because the baby wasn't his.

Pulling back into traffic, he headed for the turnoff.

Claire hadn't changed at all. Nothing had. She didn't like the way something was going and shut him out. No chance to argue. No chance to make his case.

But he'd be damned if he'd let things end the same, with another polite phone call and the entire country between them. To hell with that.

CHAPTER TWENTY-ONE

CLAIRE was tired. Weak. Aching to give in to the fatigue that plagued her on too many levels to count. She'd relented and let Sally in for a few hours, after the girl had planted herself on her doorstep bellowing about getting the police involved if Claire didn't open up and prove she was still alive.

She'd opened the door and braved Sally's shock and outrage at finding her still in the pajamas she'd slept in the night before, eyes swollen and hair knotted in some unholy mess.

"That rat bastard did this to you!"

And then Claire had been forced to explain that Ryan was not, in fact, a rat bastard. But that they were through regardless.

Sally had sat with her, quietly for a while, and then listening when Claire talked. She'd brought some gourmet soup and reheated it while Claire showered, refusing to go until half a bowl had been consumed.

And then she'd been alone again. The way she'd wanted it. Except alone, there was nothing to prevent her mind from revisiting all the moments she'd allowed herself to go astray. All the opportunities untaken, where she might have held herself apart but instead gave in to the feel-good temptation of what Ryan offered. And with each passing hour it worsened.

She wanted to go to sleep, but somehow the idea of lying in that bed where Ryan had held her was too much to bear.

Eventually, her eyes closed and her head rested against the arm of the couch and she gave herself over to the bliss of numb.

Three hard raps sounded at her door some time later, jolting her to her feet as she grasped the panels of her robe together in a disoriented rush. For an instant the fog of confusion kept reality at bay, but then another bout of knocking had the here and now slamming securely into place.

Ryan.

He'd said he was on his way, but that was before she'd told him it was over. He shouldn't have come, but even as she thought it, her heart gave an unsteady lurch toward the door.

"Open up, Claire." The words came low and rough through the wood panels dividing them, warning her he was a man past patience. After a flight that was at minimum five and a half hours, plus whatever it took to make that flight happen, he'd have to be.

Throwing the lock, she'd barely turned the knob when he'd pushed the door open, caught her hip and backed her down the hall, kicking the door closed behind him.

Gasping at the unexpected contact as much as at the sight of Ryan's haggard features, she clutched at his sleeves for balance. "What are you doing here? I told you not to come—"

"I heard you," he said, releasing her into the corner as he jerked free of his coat at the small closet.

Her heart was racing, her throat tight from too much emotion over too many hours. "Then why?"

Ryan turned a caustic smile on her. "Come on. Like you really don't know?"

Her head shook in willful denial.

"Closure," he answered, jerking his tie to loosen and then starting on the buttons down his shirt. "What we've been after from the start."

"No," she whispered in strangled protest.

His fingers stilled at the fourth button, his dark eyes narrowing on her as she stared at the wide swath of tanned skin and smattering of crisp hair already revealed.

"'No' what?" he snapped, planting a hand on the wall beside her head. Closing her in without touching her at all.

His voice lowered, dangerously softening. "It's not closure? Or closure wasn't what you were after? Or 'no,' don't stop until I've got you wrapped around me, giving up my name on a scream?"

Her breath rushed out at the angry, seductive taunt, leaving her without response.

Taking her silence for the victory it was, Ryan adjusted his stance, lowering his head so his words fell warm and wet against her ear. "Can you leave it like this, Claire... Unfinished?"

The fists that had balled at her sides were now pressed against the hard plane of his stomach.

Unfinished.

She didn't want that. Not for herself. Not for Ryan.

"I need more, Claire..." Running a light finger down the side of her neck, he followed the silk lapel of her robe to the vee where it met its partner. Hooked the panel and steadily drew it back to expose the swell of her bare breast. "...than just another empty phone call."

Cool air collided with her oversensitive skin. And then the slightly callused pad of Ryan's thumb brushed the turgid peak of her nipple, pushing a pleading whimper past her lips.

Satisfaction growled against her ear as need spilled heavy and warm through her center.

And then both his hands were on her. Cupping the growing weight of her breasts, one sheathed in silk, the other bare. Silk and rough skin contrasted in sensual harmony, pulling at the needy place in her core. "Give me tonight."

"Tonight," she moaned, arching into the teasing abrasion,

begging for more. Her own hands clutching convulsively at the sides of Ryan's shirt. She needed this. Maybe more even than he did.

Ryan's hand wound into the hair at her nape, coaxing her head back so that she had no choice but to meet his gaze. "I need to say goodbye. Don't you need it, too?"

Staring up at him, her throat tightened and suddenly she was blinking back the sting of tears.

"Yes," she whispered tentatively, moving her hands to his face. Then more boldly allowing her fingertips to trace each beloved feature. To memorize them. The sharp blade of his nose. The high ridge of his cheekbones, the thick fringe of his lashes.

Ryan's eyes closed, the tension in his body seeming to leak out with the weight of his sigh…and then gathered again as something new. Something different. Hungry.

The hand in her hair tightened, slowly pulling her head back so that she was open to him, exposed, waiting for his kiss.

Eyes drifting over the offering he'd made of her, he drew an even, controlled breath. "When I hold you tonight, I'm going to know it's the last time. I'm going to take my time over you."

As if to emphasize the point, he bent his head to her mouth and licked a slow path around her parted lips, then slid his tongue between, filling her in increments until a shudder of aching anticipation racked her captive frame and a needy groan chased his painstaking retreat.

"I'm going to make you wait, Claire." Another rough stroke of his tongue into her waiting mouth followed by the scrape of his teeth across her jaw, neck and that decadent spot beneath her ear.

Hands skating to her hips, he braced her for the steely

length of him rocking against her. "Make it last. There won't be a single inch of you I haven't tasted…touched."

Desire churned within her, turning her breath to shallow pants. Hands fumbling between them, she worked the remaining buttons down Ryan's shirt. Wrestled with his belt and fly until he caught her wrists within his hand and led her back down the hall. In her bedroom he stripped them both naked, then followed her down to the bed. "God, Claire, I need to make you mine one more time."

Claire closed her eyes as Ryan's body pressed down on her. The first moments following making love were always a decadent torture. That bit of time when he gave in to the bone-deep muscle fatigue resulting from the total attention he showered on her body. His reckless collapse. Her fingers would trail a light path over the broad terrain of his back, circling one way and then the other as she encouraged him to linger a moment longer.

But tonight was different. She clung to the broad, powerful shoulders of the man she loved, knowing with each second that passed they came closer to that final goodbye. She wanted to savor the weight of him against her. Wanted to remember the heavy beat of his heart and the dampness of his skin. The hold so secure she couldn't escape if she tried.

But too soon he pushed to an elbow and rolled to his side. A warm hand slid down her back as deep brown, contemplative eyes met hers. "Are you okay?"

"Yes." Her lips trembled as she tried to smile for him, somehow convey that he had been right. That she'd needed this goodbye too. That she felt right about it. Only, the muscles of her face rebelled, refusing to bow or stretch into a lie they didn't feel.

These were the final seconds of what she'd once dreamed would be forever.

"Maybe it doesn't have to be the end, Claire. This last week has been nuts, but think about what it was like before that."

She was. They had been too good not to want more of. Too good not to wonder if it could last. Salty emotion clogged her throat as she began to force the words she didn't want to speak from it. "Neither of us were looking for forever. Just an affair, because we'd tried marriage and...look where it left us. Right?"

It was as close as she could come to asking him for the words they'd stopped saying nine years ago. The promises that everything would be okay. That they could make it through.

As close as she would allow herself to come to believing in *maybe*.

His hand stilled, then resumed its repetitive stroke as he leaned in, pressing his lips to her brow. "Right." A tight breath filled the space between them, then, "Just say it."

Closing her eyes, she swallowed past all the wrong words that kept pushing to get free.

Shaking her head, she whispered, "I don't know how."

All she knew was that her heart was breaking with every savage beat and she was terrified she'd already let herself fall too far. That she'd never be able to piece herself back together.

Ryan cupped her cheek and, tipping her face to his, brushed the thick pad of his thumb across her tear-streaked skin. A wry smile twisted his lips. "No one should go through a divorce without having their heart shredded, right? Even if the heartbreak is almost a decade old, signing away that promise of a life together should make it fresh. It shouldn't be easy."

"No. It shouldn't. It isn't."

His lips met hers in a gentle clasp. Held as he gathered her close for one final embrace in a marriage of fools.

And then it was over.

CHAPTER TWENTY-TWO

"ARE you sure about this?" Sally asked, her concern weighing as heavily as the delicate burden balanced between Claire's fingertips.

It was a small lacquered box, constructed of wood so thin, it threatened to crumble under even the most careful touch. Claire didn't look at it often. Seldom allowed herself to even think about it tucked into that safe corner, deep in the recesses of her walk-in closet. But it was there. This little treasure box of broken dreams.

Tucking one leg beneath her, she sat at the edge of the bed and opened the lid. As always, the sight of the few items within pulled at the dark places in her soul, freeing a destructive love that made her want to clutch the box tight to her chest until it shattered against her heart.

Sally settled across from her, carefully steadying the box as her slight weight shifted the mattress. Then, with one finger, she stroked the pale green nubs of a single half-finished bootie nestled within and whispered, "Soft."

The hushed word, both caring and reverent, loosened something within Claire and she smiled across at her friend. "Isn't it? This was my great-aunt's pattern and her hook." Then pulling up a layer of tissue, she withdrew a photo and passed it across to Sally, who gingerly held it by the edges.

"Oh, wow, is that you?" she asked, pointing to the twelve-year-old version of the woman before her. "Your family is beautiful."

They were. And the love she'd felt when that family snapshot had been taken was beautiful too. She'd never believed it to be a conditional thing, or that the possibility of that love being revoked could exist.

She'd been so naive on so many counts.

After carefully replacing the photo, Claire moved on to what she'd come for. A slender platinum band, worn thin at the base, and channel set with five diamond chips. Ryan's grandmother's wedding ring.

Her wedding ring.

She could still feel Ryan sliding that symbol of eternity over her fourth finger. Still feel that hollow pit opening in her belly when she realized it didn't belong there.

"You don't have to do this, Claire. I mean, did he even ask for it?"

She shook her head. Ryan would never ask for it back, but that didn't mean he shouldn't have it. The ring belonged in his family. Whether he married again or not. And returning it with the papers seemed like the appropriate thing to do.

"I've held on to it long enough." It was time she let go.

Sally snapped open the lid on a small black velvet box they'd picked up at the jeweler's that morning.

Fingering the delicate band one last time, Claire felt the cool trail of a tear slip down her cheek. Surprised, she laughed, wiping it away.

"Claire?"

Waving off Sally's growing concern, she set the band against its silk pillow and closed the box. "I'll be fine. I was before. I will be again."

Maybe if she said it enough times, eventually she'd start to believe it.

* * *

"So what do you think?"

Ryan's head snapped up and his stare locked on Ty Baker, the man seated across the conference table. Then shot over to Denis, who signaled with the barest nod as an IM popped up on the open laptop in front of him.

"You called it. They're willing to give on every point, except the water rights."

Thank God for Denis. The man didn't let anything slip past, including his jackass boss taking a brain break in the middle of high-stakes negotiations.

"Ty, I think we can work something out. Let me go over the new numbers and we'll talk Monday."

"Fair enough." They pushed back from their seats and met at the door to shake hands. "This one's going to make us a lot of money, Brady."

Yeah, if only Ryan could care enough about it to keep his focus until the deal closed.

Once the Baker team departed, Denis turned a cool eye on him.

"It won't happen again," he answered to the unspoken *What the hell?* Denis was shooting him.

"Are you sure? I've never seen you drop the ball like that. Not after thirty hours of negotiations, not ever."

Ryan's molars ground down as his jaw clenched in self-directed frustration. "I know." Like he knew his performance affected people beyond himself. He had to get it together. Had to stop spiraling into that *state of Claire* he couldn't quite break free from.

Denis blew out a breath and scanned the ceiling, looking more out of his element than Ryan had ever seen him.

Oh, come on. Denis couldn't quit.

Okay, he'd messed up today, but they'd been together for seven years. "Something else you want to say, Denis?"

"I realize these last few weeks have been difficult for you.

And I'm wondering—" the man actually pulled at his collar before turning a strained, sympathetic eye on him "—if you'd like to…talk about it."

Hell. No.

Ryan wanted to puke. Denis, his hard-hitting, all-business rock of an assistant was not asking him if he needed a hug and some ice cream.

"That bad?"

Denis weighed the question long enough to where the answer was obvious.

"Forget I asked. Get me the revised offer for Baker and then take off."

At Denis's nod and quick exit, Ryan headed back to his office.

After a few minutes the email arrived with the updated file, Ryan's schedule for the coming week, and a notice that the settlement agreement had been dropped off for Claire's signature.

He'd known the papers would be delivered today. Had been telling himself it was a good thing. That once they were signed, he'd be able to put her behind him. Close his eyes without seeing the smile that was heartbreak, acceptance and longing all wound into one as Claire had watched that little boy in her studio. Her hair whipping like black ribbons in the wind as she crouched above a tide pool, marveling at the starfish she'd found within. He'd stop dreaming of her each night, reaching for her every morning and taking it like a slug to the gut when he remembered what they had wasn't what either of them wanted and that the sultry moans and breathless laughter were only echoes of a time come and gone.

For him.

One of these days, she'd be giving them to someone else. She'd move on to some chump who'd been ready, waiting in the wings. Because that's what strong, intelligent, sexy, alluring women did when they finally put their past behind them.

That's what he wanted for her, so why the hell did he want to drive down to New York, foot to the floor, and stake out her place. Just lie in wait to sabotage the next guy who thought to press for a kiss or a laugh or a smile or one instant of her attention.

Damn it, what was wrong with him!

Shoving away from his desk, the schedules and the deals he'd been counting on to work him into an emotional oblivion that hadn't come, Ryan stalked to the window.

It was staying light later these days and the city of Boston was spread out beneath him in evening's muted glow. Cabs and cars cut through the streets as the sidewalks emptied of suits and began filling with style. Women laughing as they headed out for a night on the town. Couples walking together, some holding hands, others simply creating an intimacy between them identifiable even from four floors above.

He and Claire had walked these streets. They'd gotten dinner at a popular restaurant a few blocks down. Spent the night making plans. They'd been so damn happy then. He'd had *everything*. A career on the rise. A wife he loved. Their child on the way. Looking back now, though, all he could see was what he'd been about to lose. Everything that mattered.

He wondered if he could go back to the kid he'd been and warn himself about the failures, the heartbreak and the futility that fate had in store for him, if he'd have been willing to give up those good times with Claire to spare himself that future. If he'd have been willing to cut that time short by even one day.

No. Because the kid he'd been then hadn't yet learned how to quit. Or fail. Or stop trying. And sure as hell not when it came to something as important as what he had with Claire.

Hell, even after his firsthand experience with all the pain, years later he'd tried again—

The thought stopped him cold.

Was that what he'd been doing, trying again?

No, it had been an affair. Attraction. Chemistry. *Closure*...

Because on some level he still hadn't let himself believe it was over.

On some level, he didn't want to let her go. At all. Which was why at every opportunity he'd had to maintain a modicum of distance between them, he'd instead pulled her closer. Found a way to further infiltrate all the parts of her life she'd tried to deny him access to. Her home. The gallery. Those last dark secrets of her past.

And maybe that was why Claire's shutting him out again— giving him that taste of history repeating itself he just couldn't swallow—had made him so nuts. Pushed him to the point where he couldn't let her go without burning across the country to demand something more.

Only, when she'd actually given him *more*, given him that last chance to tell her he wanted something real, he'd been too lost in the pain and the past and his failures and fears to take it.

A violent curse tore out of him as he stalked across the office, slammed a hand against the wall and closed his eyes.

What the hell was he doing?

CHAPTER TWENTY-THREE

HER eyes had glazed over again, her focus lost in the ether with all the dreams, memories and fantasies she used to tell herself she couldn't have. Blinking back into focus, Claire pushed pen to paper, ignoring the clench of her stomach as she initialed yet another paragraph.

No second-guessing. No going back.

Only, at the last page a tremor shook the pen free of her grasp and she found herself gulping air as she dashed for the open window across the room. All the doubts she'd worked to stifle crowded in at once, threatening to suffocate her.

Forearms resting on the pane, she hung her head, taking long draws of the cool New York night air and an inventory of the sounds that filled it. Car doors thudding. Shouts and greetings. Laughter and sirens. The wind rushing over the building walls.

Closing her eyes, she waited for the calm that inevitably followed the storm of her emotions. A calm that was preempted by the deep call of her name cutting through the night.

She jerked back, bumping hard against the open window as she gaped down at the walk where Ryan stood, hand on his head, muttering a curse about her being careful.

Yes, careful. With her heart. With her head. With her hope.

God, what was he doing there?

Within seconds Ryan was back in her apartment, standing in the same hallway where he'd claimed his last goodbye. Only this time, as he held her, it was to probe at what proved to be a very tender bump on the head.

Cradling her temples between his palms, Ryan searched her face. "Are you okay?"

No. Not at all. Not with him standing so close she could barely breathe or think or keep from reaching out to stroke the stubbled edge of his jaw. "I'm fine."

Ryan nodded once, his thumb brushing the rise of her cheekbone.

"So strong," he murmured into the air between them in a way that made it sound as though the reassurance had been for himself. And with sudden crushing clarity, she understood why he'd come.

Because the papers had been delivered today and he'd needed to know that she could handle it. She'd thought she could. But that was before Ryan stood in front of her brushing a brutal stroke of reality across her face.

Defensively she took a step back. Crossed her arms over her chest and pushed a smile she didn't feel to her lips. "I am strong."

Maybe they both needed to be reminded of it.

"I know and—" The expression on his face was one she didn't recognize. He looked almost vulnerable in that second before he glanced away, clearing his throat as he pushed the fallen strands of his dark hair back from his brow. "Are those the papers? You signed them?"

Claire's stomach turned sick as she watched him take that first step toward the kitchen counter where she'd been working. Panic surged and she pushed past him, quickly gathering the documents into a haphazard pile against her chest.

"I was nearly finished," she said, trying again to sound

confident. Wishing she'd just taken the stack and signed them the second they'd arrived. Returned them instead of—

"What the hell is this?" The savage growl cut through her thoughts, snapping her attention back to Ryan and the murderous expression on his face.

Terrified, Claire scanned the counter expecting to see one of the settlement pages inadvertently left behind. But there was nothing. Nothing to explain the cold rage shining in his eyes.

Nothing except a black jeweler's box straining within his fist.

"This is how you're moving on?" he roared, his shoulders and chest seeming to broaden impossibly wider as he rounded the counter, closing in on her until she'd backed herself against the sink, too stunned to respond.

"Who is he?" he demanded, looking for all the world as though he were about to tear the building down around them.

"Ryan, it's my ring."

No kidding, Claire! He'd seen a ring box before. He just hadn't expected to see one sitting beside their divorce documents. Whoever he was hadn't wasted a goddamn second. But it couldn't be too late. He wouldn't let it. He just had to know who he was up against and then— "It's that Aaron, isn't it?" He ground out the words. It had to be. And to think he'd passed him off as not being any kind of threat at all. He wanted to find that slick bastard and take him apart limb by limb.

But then Claire's hands were his, pulling at his fingers so she could open the box. Push it in front of his face.

And then there it was.

Claire's wedding band.

Everything slowed. Quieted. Calmed.

He hadn't seen it in years. Hadn't let himself wonder about

when, exactly, she'd stopped wearing it. Hadn't given himself license to acknowledge anything beyond the fact that one day he opened the *Times* to her picture and it was gone.

But here it was again.

Slim. Almost insubstantial as he withdrew it from its silk pillow and tested it in the palm of his hand. Funny how in his mind there'd been so much more to this little band. He'd sworn he could feel the weight of it heavy and solid against his chest as he'd stood before the justice of the peace waiting to give it to Claire.

Ryan's brow drew down as he followed the delicate band with his fingertip. "I'm sorry. For this insanity just now. For the last two months. Hell, for the past nine years."

Claire's hand smoothed over his chest, stilled at that spot above his heart, reserved just for her. "Are *you* okay?"

Ryan shook his head, let out a short laugh as he met the blue eyes peering up at him. Saw the concern. The confusion. "Do I seem okay?"

Claire's quiet laugh answered his own. "No."

Looking down, he realized that he'd crowded her against the sink. The divorce papers had spilled around their feet and even now his legs were pressed against hers.

Stepping back, he briefly touched her hand. "I don't think I've been okay since the day I let you go. The day I lost the part of myself that knew how to fight for what mattered. But I was so blinded by my fear of failing you—us—again, I couldn't even try."

"*You* didn't fail." The hand at his chest bunched into his shirt, making him smile.

His little Claire, once again using her brute strength to push him around. If she didn't want to let him go, he wouldn't move an inch.

But he wouldn't let her ignore the truth either.

"Are you still my wife, Claire?" he asked, the words

scraping raw from his throat. "Are you living in my house, sharing your life with me? Do we have the children and the laughter and the love I promised?"

Her face was pale now, her eyes haunted. But she wouldn't look away. "I'm the one who left. None of this was you."

His voice hardened as the guilt and shame ate through him. "You're wrong. Nine years, Claire. Nine years you gave me to come after you. But I was too much of a coward to do it. And too selfish to let you go completely."

Claire closed her eyes, shook her head. "No."

"You could have served me with papers six years ago, Claire. Sent this ring back to me then. But you held on to it all this time. Because I'd promised you forever and even though I'd let you down, somehow, you still believed in it."

She was trembling now. Her lips had parted and soft puffs of her breath were washing over his knuckles where he held his hand over hers. He wanted to kiss her. Sink into her mouth and tell himself she was his. Only, he didn't know if she could be.

"When you left, I made excuses. I told myself you were too fragile for me to fight. That if I pushed you to stay, you'd break under the pressure. But you're not fragile anymore and I'm done making excuses. You're strong."

The muscles worked up and down her throat. Once, twice, before she found the words to ask, "What are you saying?"

"I love you, Claire. And I'm going to fight for you."

Heart slamming in his chest, Ryan watched as Claire absorbed his words and then slowly stepped out of his hold. Seemingly dazed, she knelt down and began collecting the papers littering the floor at their feet.

Ryan ducked down beside her, reaching for her hands to still them. Panic rising at her lack of response, he tried to catch her eyes, but she was blinking back her tears and so he just said what he needed her to hear.

"I know I don't deserve another chance, but I want it anyway. Because I know I can make you happy. I'll spend the rest of my life proving it to you." He swallowed hard, working past his pride, because this time it was his turn to lay himself bare and put himself on the line. Take the risk, because Claire was all the reward he could ask for. "You can sign those papers, Claire. If you want, I'll sign them too. But I still won't give up on us. I'll fight for you until I win you back. Nine years or nineteen. I won't quit."

Claire ran her fingers over the documents at his feet. "You'd sign this?"

His jaw ground down, but he nodded. "Yes." And began scooping the pages up. He'd do whatever it took to make her happy. And maybe that agreement was enough, because a tremulous smile broke across Claire's lips.

"Then I guess I didn't ask for enough."

Didn't ask for enough? This from the woman he'd had to strong-arm into taking anything. His gaze dropped to the documents in his hands and the bits of blue ink littering the pages. She'd modified the agreement and was asking for...

"A helicopter and pilot," he coughed out, surprised but not unwilling to accommodate the request until he noted the qualifier following. "On standby in every state?"

Claire pushed to her feet. "To start."

Following her progress back to the living room with his eyes, he had to ask, "Are you drunk?"

A clear blue gaze shot back at him, elusive and intriguing. But not without the echoes of hurt and hope from the moments before. "Are you rejecting my counter?"

A knot of tension bound around his chest began to slip. "No."

Her brow furrowed as she stopped beside the couch. "Then keep reading."

The next paragraph listed another amendment. "My L.A.

office building?" Something hot and powerful began to build deep within, growing more intense with each neatly scrawled notation. "A pool boy for your New York apartment, which, incidentally, does not have a pool. A whale. A yacht. The beach house. Live-in masseuse…and, of course, one for Sally, too. And this is just page two." Ryan was on his feet, closing in fast. "Greedy thing, aren't you."

"Someone must have spoiled me."

The breath raced from his lungs as he caught Claire around the waist with a single arm and pulled her against him, felt the racing of her heart against his. "I'll spoil you for the rest of your life, kitten. Just explain this first."

He needed to hear the words. Needed to know without question they were on the same page.

A soft pink rose to her cheeks and, hesitantly, she glanced away. "Until the settlement is finalized, we continue as lovers."

"Claire…" Her name came gravel rough from a throat choked with emotion. Catching her chin with the crook of his finger, he brought those beautiful blues back to him.

Claire once again found herself blinking back tears, but these were tears born of sweet joy rather than sorrow. He loved her. Wanted her. Had come back to fight for her. "So unless you want to know how many small islands I've *asked for…* strip."

"Strip?"

The smile that split his face melted her knees and left her clinging to the powerful chest and shoulders supporting her.

"This was your plan?"

"Well, we had a deal." And she'd realized she'd rather have risked her heart than give up the man she loved forever.

That exuberant smile shifted, eased, as his eyes held hers. "We did," he agreed, brushing a strand of hair behind her ear. Gathering her closer, he stepped over to the couch and pulled her down into his lap. Pressed his brow to hers and took her hand in his. "But the one I'm thinking of was forever…"

Her eyes closed at the words so powerful the sound of them was nearly more than she could bear.

"It included vows." He pulled her hand to his lips, kissed each fingertip, every knuckle. "And a ring."

Her eyes opened as Ryan held her slender platinum band before her.

"Ryan." His name broke from her lips on a quiet sob that was relief, hope, elation, surrender and love all in one. So much love.

"I want you to wear this, Claire. I want it to mean forever. But if you need time—"

Only then her hands were in his hair, her words rushing over his lips between each kiss. "I love you…I love you…I love you…Forever. Always."

Ryan broke back, a dark intensity blazing in his eyes. "It nearly killed me, losing you once, Claire. I won't let it happen again. I can't promise you a fairy tale. But I can promise that no matter what comes our way, I'll be by your side through it."

Sliding the band over the fourth finger of her left hand, he spoke her words back to her. A vow renewed. "Always. Forever. I love you."

* * * * *

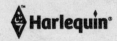

ALWAYS POWERFUL, PASSIONATE AND PROVOCATIVE

Harlequin® Desire delivers
strong heroes, spirited heroines
and compelling love stories.

Harlequin Desire features
your favorite authors, including

ANN MAJOR, DIANA PALMER, MAUREEN CHILD AND BRENDA JACKSON.

Passionate, powerful and provocative
romances *guaranteed!*

For superlative authors, sensual stories
and sexy heroes, choose Harlequin Desire.

www.ReaderService.com

 HARLEQUIN® HISTORICAL
Where love is timeless

*Imagine a time of chivalrous knights
and unconventional ladies,
roguish rakes and impetuous heiresses,
rugged cowboys and
spirited frontierswomen—
these rich and vivid tales
will capture your imagination!*

HARLEQUIN HISTORICAL...
THEY'RE TOO GOOD TO MISS!

...there's more to the story!

Superromance.
A *big* satisfying read about unforgettable characters. Each month we offer *six* very different stories that range from family drama to adventure and mystery, from highly emotional stories to romantic comedies—and much more! Stories about people you'll believe in and care about. Stories too compelling to put down....

Our authors are among today's *best* romance writers. You'll find familiar names and talented newcomers. Many of them are award winners—and you'll see why!

If you want the biggest and best in romance fiction, you'll get it from Superromance!

Exciting, Emotional, Unexpected...

A *Romance* FOR EVERY MOOD™